Traveling Left of Center and Other Stories

NANCY CHRISTIE

Traveling Left of Center and Other Stories

Nancy Christie

To my father, Joseph V. Ress

Table of Contents

Introduction:
Afraid of the Dark

The short story ain't what it used to be. Neither is being a writer. The pride that literary lights used to take in being writers is gone with the Internet, Reality TV, 140-character communication, the well-documented short attention span, the well-recognized dumbing down of our culture. A sort of Song of Roland is heard in the literary land. (And if that reference escapes you, Google it.)

I should say immediately that I am a serious admirer of Nancy Christie's work. She is by no means a new writer. (Like so many wordsmiths, most of her work over the years has been journeyman stuff; she has led the freelance writer/teacher life that so many literary folk are forced to live in these post-literary days.) But if she is not a new writer, her short stories are new writing. Exciting new writing.

The short story, like the poem, is a tough buck. And much as some of us may long for the cultures and days of living, breathing O. Henrys, Guy de Maupassants, Katherine Mansfields and Ernest Hemingways, this sort of literary endeavor, this art form, is pretty much the creature of obscure and non-descript periodicals whose names end in "Quarterly" or "Review" (The Past) or very, very strange names (apparently from The Future).

Nancy Christie's stories are amazing. The world she shows us is a terrifying world of deluded, demented people. The sort of people who never get a second look or a second thought from you and me, but whose lives are nightmares. These nondescript, unbearably fragile people are, she makes us discover, everywhere, either fearing danger where none exists or failing to see the shadow of the doom that falls across their paths. Often their most ardent wish is a death wish. And what is more terrifying, often when they get their wish, they welcome it.

The world of Nancy Christie's short stories is a world of both the sudden gratuitous cruelty as well as the prolonged torture that human beings inflict upon each other and upon themselves.

It is a world peopled primarily by desperate, helpless women, sinking into their own deadly quicksand (though there is an occasional feckless man in there somewhere). These short stories are the chronicles of these people's inevitable individual defeats.

And if all of this sounds dreadful, why praise the writer? Because her world has been so well hidden from us that when she reveals it, we catch our breath as the first readers of Poe or Kafka or the darker passages of Mark Twain's later works surely must have gasped.

Her world is so real! And just when you think— by which I mean desperately try to escape it through disbelief—"This can't be!"—a sudden, strange and surprising detail pops up in a strange and surprising place and you are pulled back into facing the truth.

There are writers who are wonderful because they make you say to yourself, "Yes, that's how it is!" Then there is Nancy Christie, whose writing makes you say,

"So—that's how it is..." You say it with the wonder and dismay of a reader discovering proof of what life is for the secret few—and, you realize with new-found terror, what life can be for all of us.

That is why Nancy Christie is a wonderful writer.

Morrow Wilson, novelist,
*David Sunshine: A Novel of the
Communications Industry*

Traveling Left of Center

"Girl," my mama had said to me the minute she entered my hospital room, "on the highway of life, you're always traveling left of center."

Mama was always saying things like that. She had a phrase for every occasion and would pronounce them with a certainty that I accepted as gospel in my younger days. But that time, I didn't pay her no mind. I just went on painting my nails Passionate Purple, hoping that the sexy polish would catch the doctor's eye.

I was justifiably proud of my hands, especially since, at that particular time, they were the only part of me that was skinny. A girl's body sure takes a beating from having a baby. It took me at least a year to get my shape back after I had Robert Nicholas, and it looked like Rebecca Nicole wouldn't be any kinder to her mama than her big brother had been.

I truly love my babies even though life would've been a lot simpler if I hadn't gotten pregnant. I would've been able to do something with my life—like go to beauty school—instead of changing diapers and cleaning baby spit-up for days on end.

It was hard being a mother with no husband to lean on. But to give Mama her due, from the beginning she was right there ready to help me out.

"You're having a baby?" The way Mama shrieked when I told her the news, you'd think she had never heard of it before. Granted, I *was* going to make her a grandma at the same time I became a mother, but I didn't know why it was such a big surprise. Bobby and I had been keeping company for at least six months before I got pregnant.

"Good Lord, what will I say to the ladies at bingo?" Bingo was my mama's one passion. She never missed bingo night at the church. "They're going to ask me how it happened and what will I *say*?"

"Well, if they don't know how it happens by now, they're pretty damn stupid," I had snarled back and then ran into the bathroom to lose what was left of my breakfast, thanks to the endless bouts of morning sickness.

All in all, though, Mama took it really well. Even when Bobby left me two months before the Big Event, she didn't say too much, beyond the expected, "Well, I told you he was no good. He had shifty eyes. I saw that right away."

Maybe she was right. I don't know if I ever noticed his eyes. I was too busy looking at his sexy half-smile and the way his shoulders filled out those white T-shirts he wore. His arms were so full of muscles that he could barely fold his sleeve over the pack of unfiltered Camels he was always smoking.

Bobby had a way of blowing smoke out of the corner of his mouth that made me weak at the knees. So how could I refuse him? I never thought I'd get pregnant, not that fast anyway. It wasn't like I planned it or anything, although I did picture the two of us in a little apartment with ruffled curtains and a new bedroom set from Furniture Plus.

So, it really wasn't my fault. Little Robert Nicholas just happened. That was what I told Mama.

"Things don't 'just happen,'" Mama snapped. "Girl, you can't do now and think later. You've got to pay attention!"

Mama was always preaching at me, always telling me how I needed to pay attention. Like that night when the policeman stopped me and Mary Jean Macabobby. All we did was go to the neighborhood bar after work for a few beers before we headed home.

I figured I was okay to drive since we only had to go a few blocks and nobody was out that late anyway. Nobody except the cops, I mean, and when I heard the siren, I knew I was in trouble. But I still swear that light was yellow when I went through it.

Luckily, he was best friends with Mary Jean's big brother and let me off with a lecture and a ticket for an expired license.

"Who looks at their driver's license?" I wailed, trying to get sympathy from him. But he just shook his head.

Then Mary Jean poked me in the ribs and hissed, "Shut up before he smells the beer on your breath," and I clammed up pretty fast. Besides, my words were slurring a bit.

But he could have given us a break. It wasn't like I did it on purpose. And I did look especially nice, too, with my hair all curly and my nails painted Russian Roulette Red—the latest shade, according to the manicurist at Nails-To-Go.

But that didn't cut no ice with him. He didn't even bat an eye when I let my fingertips rest on his when he handed me the ticket.

When I asked Mama for money to pay the fine, she gave it to me with a half-hour lecture along with it. "Don't you know about drinking and driving? What if there had been an accident? You could've ended up in jail if he hadn't been a friend of Mary Jean's brother. You were just *lucky*! But you can't count on luck *all* the time!" she said. "Girl, you've *got* to start paying attention!"

She wouldn't let me drive the Buick on my own after that, which was how I ended up with Bobby. He had a candy-apple red Oldsmobile with seats covered in fake fur. That was where we did it the first time. Even now, my heart beats faster when I see a car with plushy seat covers.

So, in a funny kind of way, it was Mama's fault that I got pregnant. And the fault of that policeman.

But Mama came around in the end. She threw me a baby shower and bought me a set of sheets with puppies and kittens printed on them for the secondhand crib that Mary Jean's aunt gave me. The only time Mama got a little testy was when I unwrapped a shower present from one of the girls at work: a sexy black nightgown with ruffles down the front along with a gift card that said, "For later."

"There better not be no 'later,'" Mama answered really fast with a warning shake of her head. "She's got enough on her plate for now."

I just ignored her, holding it up to me, but the nightgown barely covered my belly. I had gained almost forty pounds with that baby and couldn't imagine sliding that nightie over my hips any time soon.

In fact, it was almost twelve months to the day before I could wear it without looking ridiculous. But when I did, Randy's eyes damn near popped out of his head. It made all those hours of belly crunches worthwhile.

I had met Randy when I ran into the new Quik Mart for baby formula. The store had just opened up, and Randy was in charge of hiring clerks and ordering merchandise. That was what he did all over the county: set up new convenience stores and make sure he offered what the customers needed.

"You sure took care of my needs," I used to tease him when we would be alone in his motel room, hot and sweaty after making love.

"I've got plenty more in stock," he would shoot back and then we would start all over again, hugging and kissing like there was no tomorrow.

Randy was always telling me how pretty I was, how my hair was so soft and my body so sexy. I was pretty vain about my hair, and my nails too. I kept them long and polished, even though Mama said I would poke the baby's eyes out someday.

But she agreed to watch the baby when Randy and I went out. Maybe she thought he'd marry me and take the two of us off her hands. I didn't have the heart to tell her that Randy already had a wife, although he told me they weren't living together and that he would divorce her as soon as his youngest child was in school. But that was three years away and, in the meantime, all he could give me was his undying affection. And another baby.

"For God's sake, girl, don't you have enough problems?"

Mama was fit to be tied when I told her I was expecting again. Randy had sworn he was fixed, that after the last kid his wife made him have an operation.

"It must have come undone, honey," he said, his big brown eyes looking into mine. "You know how I feel about you. Please tell me you forgive me."

What could I say? In the end, I let him off the hook and told him it would all work out. And it would have too except for the fact his wife called him at work one day and said little Joey missed his daddy and would he please come home for the sake of the children.

So, he went, leaving me three months along. Mama just shook her head and then hauled out the infant clothes that she had packed away when Robert Nicholas outgrew them.

At least my second pregnancy was easier. No morning sickness and I kept my weight gain under twenty-five pounds. Doctor Bill said I was doing real well. He was new in town and real cute, with curly brown hair and baby blue eyes.

One weekend, I had my hair cut short and tinted auburn, and when he saw me at the next check-up, his mouth kind of dropped open for a second. I must admit that it felt great to get under a man's skin even at five months along.

After that, I always made sure I looked my best for my visits, even spritzing on some Night Moves cologne just before he would come into the room.

Luckily, when my time came, he was out of town and some old doctor delivered me. I say "luckily" because there is no time a woman looks her worst than when she's spread-eagled on a table with her unshaved legs up high, straining and groaning to give birth.

They even took off my nail polish, which is why I was putting on a fresh coat when Mama came to see her second grandchild and give me her latest lecture.

"You are an accident waiting to happen," she continued, while I waited for the first coat to dry. If I hurried, the polish would bubble and chip. There was nothing sexy about bubbling polish. "Here you are with two babies and no husband. What's wrong with you, anyway?"

"What do you think of the name Rebecca Nicole?" I asked, more to change the subject than get her opinion. I had already made up my mind. Both of my kids would have the same initials—RNR—because I used my maiden name on their birth certificate. Robert Nicholas Ryan and now Rebecca Nicole Ryan.

RNR made me think of R&R, the army's term for rest and relaxation. Or was it recreation? Well, I had had plenty of the latter, and at least while I was in the hospital, I'd get a little rest.

Once my nails were done, I had set my hair in hot rollers so when Doctor Bill came in, I'd look real good. Most women looked like hell after they had their babies. Their faces were all red, and their eyes were puffy. They smelled, too—of sweat, blood, and antiseptic. The first thing I did after I had my babies was sneak out to the showers and wash away every bit of that smell. Then I shaved my legs and underarms, put on scented powder, and brushed my teeth.

With my hair done and my nails polished, I looked damn good, except for my sagging belly. But the nightgown hid most of that, and soon the crunches would make it disappear for good.

"Mama," I asked again, "how about the name?"

"Well," she started to say doubtfully, but then Doctor Bill came in and asked her to leave so he could examine me.

I didn't care too much for the look she gave me—all-knowing and warning rolled into one—but I blew her a kiss and told her to give it to Robert Nicholas when she got back home.

"Oh, Doctor, I miss my boy so," I said as he took out his stethoscope. "It's so hard to be a single mother these days."

I moved the neck of my gown a bit so he could hear my heartbeat. One thing having babies did was give me a Class A set of breasts. Since I didn't nurse, they never sagged either, but instead were firm and full. Men look at boobs before they look at bellies, so it was in my best interest to take good care of mine.

Doctor Bill wasn't much different from any other man in spite of being in the medical profession, and I swear his hand shook just a little when he held the stethoscope to my chest. I took care to take a nice deep breath and let my long shiny nails rest on the blanket where he could see them.

"Is everything all right?" I asked when it seemed it was taking him an awful long time to listen to my heart.

"Uh, just fine," he answered hurriedly, turning bright red.

I felt kind of bad about teasing him, especially when it would be six weeks before I could do much more than smile. But I could plan. A doctor—now, that had possibilities. Even Mama couldn't find anything wrong with that.

"Is my little girl doing all right?" I asked, all concerned as any proper mother would be. And I really was. She was as cute as a button. "I'm going to name her Rebecca," I added.

"What a coincidence," he said. "That's my mother's name," and after that, the rest, as they say, was history.

Doctor Bill and I saw each other pretty steady, although I wouldn't let him get a good look at me, if you know what I mean, until the crunches did their stuff. He was a nice guy, doing his residency at the hospital. No wife, either.

"A doctor doesn't have time for a wife," he explained, as we lay together on hot summer nights. "Later, once I'm established, I'll marry, of course," he added. "Then, there'll be time for golfing at the country club or having dinner parties. That's my plan."

It sounded good the way he said it. But somehow, I couldn't picture myself entertaining all those rich wives, mixing martinis, and serving those silly cucumber and butter sandwiches with the crusts cut off. I'd rather have a beer and pizza any day.

But I'd let him talk, and all the while I'd be curling up against him, running my fingers up and down his chest and kissing the side of his neck. Pretty soon, he'd stop talking about the future and get on with the present. For all his busy schedule, he certainly had enough energy left over for me.

Even Mama was impressed with him and willingly watched the kids when we went out to a fancy restaurant or the first-run showing at the movies. One thing about him, he sure wasn't cheap.

"Why, Doctor Bill," I would say teasingly when he brought me roses or candy, or took me out for a big steak dinner, "you sure are spoiling me!" Then I'd run my nails down his arm and he would get that glazed look on his face.

Mama even spared me the lecture on birth control, figuring that a doctor would know how to prevent babies. But when we ran out of rubbers one night and I had my sexiest nightgown on, well, what was a man to do? All the self-control in the world couldn't withstand lacy black lingerie and Tangerine Touch nail polish.

I knew his residency was almost up, but I figured he'd stay when he found out that I was pregnant. I thought his plans of being a big city doctor with a big city wife was all just talk. After all, everybody had dreams, even me. I just never figured he really believed in his.

And it isn't helping that this baby has been ornery from the start. I'm spending more time in the bathroom than anywhere else, and my belly is swelling so big you'd think I was carrying twins, although the clinic said it's too early to be sure. My face is splotchy, and my hair is stringy. No wonder he found it so easy to leave me.

I'm six months gone now, and he's gone, too—off to a bigger hospital in a bigger town. He's promised to send me money, but I'm not holding my breath.

It's a rotten shame the way these things go wrong for me. I don't do a damn thing and yet I'm always left holding the bag—or to be more accurate, the baby. It's not my fault that he didn't go to the drug store. And I didn't ask to be so damn fertile.

Mama is madder than a wet hen about all this. She says I need a keeper, not a husband, and she's threatening to glue my kneecaps together. She says that from now on if I so much as look at another man, she'll slap me silly.

She'll come around though. She always does, especially when she's holding the baby. Besides, I promised her that this time would be different. After the baby comes, I plan to take some classes so I can become a beautician.

"Then I'll do up your hair and paint your nails every week, Mama," I promised her when I brought home the pamphlet from the school. "If you watch the kids, I can finish this course in a year. Then I can work at the beauty shop down the street."

Mama just sniffed, but she didn't say she wouldn't help. I'll be home free as long as she doesn't come see the instructor. His name is Pierre, and he has the cutest French accent and wears the best cologne I have ever smelled on a man.

He says I have great potential and could look just like a model—after the baby comes, anyway.

"With your eyes and cheekbones, you'd be a natural," he said one night when I stayed late to look at some new hairstyle books.

"Oh, Pierre, you say the silliest things," I laughed, resting my newly manicured nails (Black Lace) on his arm. "Why, here I am, as big as a house! How can you think of me as a model? Land sakes, it's hot in here," and I brushed my hair away from my forehead and then unfastened the top button of my maternity smock.

Pierre was too polite to stare, but I knew my cleavage had caught his eye. My old maternity bras were barely big enough to hold me in place.

"There's so much I could do with you," he said. With the way he looked at me in the mirror, I had a suspicion that he didn't just mean my hairstyle.

Now Pierre wants to dye my hair jet black and give me a manicure. Ravishing Rose is the shade he had in mind. He's offered to do it for free. I might just let him.

Alice in Wonderland

"Alice! *Alice!* Where are you?"

Her mother's shrill voice crept up the stairs, seeping around the corners, through the cracks, and under the door like a damp chill until it found Alice, sitting cross-legged on her rumpled bed with a scratchy woolen blanket wrapped around her, holding tightly to her book.

She heard the words as though they came from a great distance, not just the floor below. But instead of responding, she kept on chewing, tearing off more bits from the pages to slip into her mouth and onto her tongue. *"Cairo... Alexandria... Mozambique... Tangiers..."*

"Alice! I want some tea!" complaining, demanding, the words pulling at Alice like a rope around her neck.

"*Nebet*, the master awaits your presence," said the servant, bowing before her with the respect due to one of great beauty and power.

"Tell him to wait," Alice answered calmly. She extended first one slim leg and then the other to allow the servant girl to free her delicate, high-arched feet from their sandals. "I will bathe first and then see him. Perhaps. Or perhaps not"—the control she wielded evident in her tone, her attitude.

Alice rose to her feet, slipping the silver bracelets from her fine-boned wrists before allowing the silk caftan to fall from her white shoulders. Then she freed her golden hair from the ribbon that kept it bound at the nape of her neck, the lustrous strands cascading down her back. The heat from the Sahara Desert permeated the room, melting her muscles and bones into a sinuous form until she was curled and waiting like a cobra. The perfumed water tempted her...

"Alice! Dammit, you get down here right now!"

One last bite, one final swallow, and then Alice reluctantly set the book back onto the shelf, the bangles and caftan vanishing as the cover closed. Twisting the dull brown strands of her thin hair into a bun, the ends damp from where she had absentmindedly chewed on them, she pinned them halfheartedly in place before leaving her narrow, dark bedroom.

She had stayed too long and the price she paid for any delay, any deviation from the daily routine was an endless litany of complaints and grievances, lasting until her mother was fed, bathed, and finally put to bed.

The schedule was set in stone, like hieroglyphics incised on the walls of an ancient tomb. Breakfast at eight, then pills, then empty the catheter bag hanging on the side of the bed of its smelly yellow liquid. Bathe the bits and pieces of a body that, each day, seemed less human and more like a shrunken mass of skin and muscle barely attached to bone.

Change the bed, bundling the dirty sheets into the washer with the requisite amount of bleach in a vain attempt to get rid of the stains and odor. Then, before she knew it, it was time to make lunch—canned tomato soup followed by a processed cheese sandwich on white bread (no variations allowed)—before she had to clean everything up again, bag and all.

Dinner. Another sponge bath. More pills. Alice didn't know where the day went, and sometimes she wondered if she too wasn't disappearing—if, with each chime of the clock at the hour, a little more of her wasn't slipping away.

At the end of the day, she'd look in the mirror, and even though she saw a face that she knew was hers—the untrimmed brown hair, the faded blue eyes with dark circles underneath, the chapped lips and sallow skin—she didn't feel *there*. It was just her reflection, nothing real. Most days, she felt as insubstantial as that mirrored image, unreality reflecting unreality into infinity—powerless, hopeless, loveless.

But when she opened her books, her world shifted and changed. It was a different reality, a glittering wonderland of power. And she was a different Alice— no longer the one being commanded, but the one doing the commanding. Men bowed before her, bearing gifts of gold and jewels and silks. Servants waited for her commands, their single goal in life to please her. She had only to lift her hand and the world was at her feet.

With each turn of the page, the walls of the old row house gave way to whatever place the words conjured up—sometimes the pyramids and temples of Egypt, sometimes the streets of Marrakesh, crowded with snake charmers and magicians. But it was always somewhere hot and dry, where the air burned her skin and enflamed her spirit. Each bite of paper took her to strange lands among strange people, the sights and sounds and smells almost (but not quite) blocking out the reality in which she lived.

If one could call it living. *If*, in fact, this was life.

"What took you so long? I've been waiting! And don't be so noisy!"

Her mother always accused her of being noisy, although Alice herself could never hear the sound of her own footsteps. She was as noiseless as a wraith, as insubstantial as a ghost. Not even the dust in the stuffy, cluttered sitting room was disturbed by her entrance.

But in her *riad* with its courtyard of fragrant flowers, she only had to breathe, and like a strong wind that one hears even in a deep sleep, her servants heard her and responded, ready to do her bidding. She would sit beside the fountains, where the fragrance of damask roses and white campion mingled in the air, and turtledoves called their mournful cry. Her presence infused the palace the way the heat from the sun infused the air. The world was hers, all hers.

"God knows I don't ask for much." The resentment in her mother's voice was reflected in her eyes. "The least you could do for an old, sick, helpless woman is to come when she needs something!"

Not much, but just the very life that coursed through Alice's veins. "I'm sorry, Mother." She plumped up the limp pillow behind the woman's back, adjusted the blanket over her lap, and gazed with a practiced eye at the glass of water and crackers. She wondered if the woman had drunk enough, eaten enough. And if she hadn't, did it matter after all?

"I've been waiting forever for my cup of tea! Where did you go?" It was always the same question, even though she knew Alice hadn't left the house but was instead trapped somewhere within its four walls.

Alice held her tongue, although there were times when she was tempted to answer her with the truth. "I was kneeling on the tasseled prayer rug in my palace in Istanbul, my head bowed to the ground, listening to the muezzin finish his morning call to prayer—'*Allah is most great. Come to prayer. Come to salvation...*' —his voice wavering in the thin clear air. A small gold and brown lizard crawled through the strands of my hair. I held his life in my hands but chose to let him survive: my power, my choice."

Or: "I was lying on the white sands at Kunduchi Bahari beach at Dar-es-Salaam. I watched the fishermen offload their catch from their dhows while my servants waited patiently to choose the freshest ones for my evening meal. And the air was filled with the screams of cormorants as they dove for the discards cast overboard."

Or: "I was walking the swarming streets of Morocco, sand-colored leather *balra* protecting my feet from the rough ground. Basket in hand and a servant at my side, I shopped the souks for lamb and spices—coriander, cumin, harissa—for the evening meal. In the distance, I heard the sound of a flute enticing the cobra to perform its swaying dance."

But instead Alice answered, "Nowhere. Do you want anything with your tea?"

"No. And I don't want tea now anyway. I changed my mind. I want something cold. Juice. Do we have any juice, or did you forget to buy it?"

Her mother knew full well that Alice had bought juice. After all, she was with Alice when the purchases were made, pulling crumpled bills and coins from her wallet, and then handing them to the cashier as if Alice couldn't be trusted to do even that one simple thing.

She never let Alice forget that it was *her* money that bought the food they ate and paid for the gas and water and electricity that they used. *Her* money that put the clothes on Alice's back and the shoes on her feet—not that Alice spent much on a wardrobe these days. Once she had given up her job to take care of her mother, she had no need for "outside clothes." That was how Alice thought of the world. It was "outside" and she was "inside," trapped forever in this house with a woman who said she was her mother but who lacked anything remotely maternal.

"When do I go to the doctor's again? Did you make the appointment like I told you to? I'm a sick old woman, you know"—as though Alice could ever forget—"and I need to see the doctor and get my pills!"

Alice hated those doctor visits: the endless delay until they were taken to the examining room, the incessant harping monologue her mother kept up while they waited for the doctor to appear, the false cheerfulness of the staff who didn't know how truly horrible her mother was.

"How good to see you, Mrs. Humphrey!" the nurse exclaimed each time, wheeling the chairbound old woman down the corridor. "How are you doing?" The feigned concern in her voice fooled Alice's mother but never Alice. This woman didn't care how her mother was doing. She was just one more in a long line of almost dead bodies.

"Oh, I'm just holding my own, but you know me, I never complain," her mother's pretense of humility and long-suffering grace grating on Alice's nerves. "I'll go when the good Lord calls me, I guess. Until then, I'll just have to be a burden to my daughter."

"Oh, I'm sure you'd never be a burden to anyone," the nurse invariably responded, helping the old woman into a gown as though it was her pleasure to provide this level of personal attention. "I'm sure your daughter is more than happy to take care of you, aren't you, dear?"

Alice never answered nor even looked up at the two of them. She didn't want to encounter the nurse's quizzical look or worse, her pity. As for her mother—the mix of malevolence and sadistic pleasure in her eyes was more than Alice could bear. She knew Alice felt trapped, *was* trapped, and took a cruel joy in implying that this parasitic arrangement could go on forever.

Instead, Alice sat on the hard plastic chair, holding her mother's cracked black leather purse, faded beige sweater, and plastic bag of pill bottles. She fantasized that *this* time the doctor would utter that longed-for word—"terminal"—that would be the key to Alice's release, her liberation. She counted the minutes until the doctor arrived, but when he did, it was always to tell her what Alice dreaded hearing: that her mother was *not* dying. Not now, not yet, and not soon enough.

"Heart sounds good. Lungs sound good," he'd report, pressing his stethoscope first against the flabby breasts, then the bony back so like a chicken's. After slipping the black blood pressure cuff around her mother's upper arm, he'd inflate it, then listen intently for the pulse of her blood through her artery.

Through it all, Alice kept her silence, simply accepting the sheaf of prescriptions that the doctor handed her. In theory, they were necessary to keep her mother alive for another thirty days. But Alice knew she didn't need them. The old woman had no intention of dying until she was good and ready.

"You're doing very well, very well indeed!" he'd say heartily as he finished making a few notes in his file with an air of importance.

Did he think he needed to justify the time he spent in the room? Alice asked herself. Did he think she cared if he took notes, performed his cursory medical exam, and wrote indecipherable words on his little notepad? The one thing she wanted from him was the promise of freedom, but *that* he was unable to offer.

"I expect you to outlast me!"—his final words falling like a life sentence on Alice's ears before he would leave the room to minister to more old people who had long since outlived their usefulness.

She just might outlive the doctor—Alice's mother was stubborn enough to do that. In any case, she'd certainly outlast Alice who, every day, was fading more and more into nothingness like the Cheshire Cat. Except it wouldn't be her smile that would be the last to go since she never smiled, hadn't smiled within this hard reality in so long that she wondered if her face muscles remembered which way to contract to make the corners of her lips turn upward. Sometimes Alice thought her mother would *never* die, but instead last forever like a vampire, draining Alice not just of blood but of life itself.

This state of affairs had been going on for so long that Alice had lost track of how many years it had been. Was it five years? Ten? Twenty? Was she thirty, forty, fifty? Had there ever been a time when she didn't spend her days and nights caring for a woman who had first given her life and then took it away, day by day, minute by minute, breath by breath?

Long ago, so long ago that she barely remembered, Alice used to leave the house. Each morning she would put on her sensible black shoes, her navy skirt, white, long-sleeved blouse, and navy jacket and take the bus into town to her job at the travel agency. There she would file papers, answer phone calls, accept packages—complete whatever task that came her way with precision and accuracy. Day after day, she would watch the clock tick away the hours of her life. Sometimes she wondered if she would be in that office until the day she died.

There *must* be something more, she would think as she handed the tickets and brochures and passport applications to the clients. There *must* be somewhere else, somewhere better, more exciting and full of life, as she accepted payments for flights and cruises and train excursions.

And there was—but not for Alice.

Now, the closest she came to traveling to faraway lands was when she slipped away to her room and opened the pages of the travel guides and atlases waiting there. Each day, she ate just a little, husbanding the pages against the time when there would be nothing left to consume. But her escape was temporary and her return inevitable, unlike her father who had escaped forever, although he had to die to do it.

Alice had found him sitting in his easy chair. His beer had spilled across his lap, soaking into the faded work pants that he wore every day although he didn't work, didn't *do* anything but twist off the caps on the bottles of malt that served as the major portion of his nourishment.

The doctor said it had been a massive heart attack and offered his reassurance that her father had died peacefully, but Alice didn't need a doctor to tell her that. How could death be anything other than peaceful since it brought a release from a life that was hardly worth living at all?

Later that night, she had eaten the entire chapter on the foods of Persia, dining on the description of thick creamy yogurt spiced with onions and cucumber, and chicken marinated in an aromatic mix of olive oil, tomatoes, and golden saffron. This was followed by *desser miveh*: a heady mix of oranges, apples, bananas, dates, and figs bathed in honey–sweet orange juice. Real food never tasted as good.

"Here's your juice." Alice handed her mother a small glass of the orange liquid. "I'll be making dinner in an hour: boiled chicken, potatoes, and parsnips."

But the only response she received was a sniff as her mother turned on the television to watch her soaps.

Alice's mother watched every episode, even going so far as to schedule her doctor visits so all she'd miss would be the morning game shows. She hated watching people win their new cars, boats, or homes. She couldn't stand all that happiness.

She never watched the news either because she didn't care what was happening in the world, only what was happening to her.

Alice stole from the room like a ghost in search of a more hospitable location to haunt and debated what to do next. Should she wash yet another load of clothes from the ever-growing pile, peel the potatoes, scrub the beige kitchen floor that never looked clean no matter how many times she washed it?

Or should she cruise the salty Mediterranean where she could watch the monk seal twist and turn in the blue waters, flashing first its soft brown back and then its spotted, creamy belly? Or climb the High Atlas to her Moroccan mountain retreat surrounded by fragrant wildflowers and sturdy walnut groves, the crystal blue sky a counterpoint to the luxuriant green vegetation?

Or should she journey to Israel to bow her head before Jerusalem's Wailing Wall, weeping over the hardships of her own life until her eyes ran dry? No, never the last. Her trips must be all pleasure, all joy, an escape from the life she lived, not a continuation of it.

The floor could wait. And if she diced the potatoes small enough, they would reach that mushy stage in time for dinner even if she started them later in the afternoon. Wash clothes then, and, while the washer was running, she might have just enough time for a camel ride across the Sahara, the wool of her long white *burnous* shielding her from the sand and sun. She would race across the desert until she reached the tent of the tribal chieftain. There they would rest together on soft pillows, dining on fruits and nuts while the spicy wine caressed their tongues, a tantalizing promise of pleasures to come.

Which book to choose? *Guide to the Sahara? North African Journeys? In the Footsteps of Desert Kings?*

So many books, acquired through the years from flea markets or taken from the small community library and never returned. Notices were sent when the books were a month, two months, three months overdue, but Alice kept writing "Moved. Left no forwarding address" on the envelopes until finally they stopped.

And it wasn't a lie, not really. When she opened the books to consume their contents—paragraph by paragraph, line by line—she *had* moved, had left the life she hated. She had gone to a place where no one could find her. No one except her mother, that is. Her voice was strong enough to transcend time and space, powerful enough to pull Alice back to this house.

Alice wanted to go *there*—*be* there—she wanted to go anywhere other than where she was right now, at this moment, in her life. But she was trapped within these walls just as the words were trapped between the covers of the books.

But little by little, there were gaps on the shelves where books once had to fight for space. The more she read—the more she consumed—the thinner the volumes became. What would she do when the pages were gone? How would she get away then? Alice didn't know, couldn't conceive of a time when she would open the books to find nothing left but empty bindings and the remains of torn-out sheets.

Don't think about it now, she told herself, choosing *Tales of Journeys to Faraway Places*. She focused on the feel of the blanket, the jolting rhythm of the camel's gait, and the sensual pleasures that awaited her. Don't be *here*, don't stay *here*. Like Alice lost in Wonderland, she must take one bite and then another, not to be smaller but rather to leave this place, quickly, quickly...

"Alice! Where are you? Get down here right now and help me!"

Alice chewed a little faster, not waiting for the pieces to turn into soft mush in her mouth but swallowing them with a great convulsive gulp. But it wasn't working. There was no camel ride, no desert sand, no dark-eyed chieftain. Her mother's voice— that cold, almost tangible thing—stood between her and the bright hot land.

Somewhere else then... She flipped the pages until she came to Greece, the land of gods and goddesses. Tearing a half-sheet section, she swallowed it quickly, and could very nearly taste the dry piney-flavored *retsina* that filled her glass. It was late afternoon, and she could almost smell the heady mix of thyme and lemons in the air. Washed through with that peculiar brilliant hot light that existed only in Greece, Alice felt as white and dry as the plastered homes dotting the hillside above the Aegean Sea, as the bones lying entombed in a Greek *nekrotafeio*.

As she tore off another piece, the cry came again. "Alice! I spilled the juice! Get down here and clean it up and bring me more!"

The more she chewed, the farther away the voice became, but when she swallowed, when her mouth was empty of the places of escape, the distance disappeared.

"Alice! I need to go to the bathroom right now! If you make me wait, there'll be a mess and you'll have to clean it. Get down here right now, dammit!"

Where had the *taverna* gone? What had happened to the sun and the blue water? She was back again in this house, too soon, far too soon.

"I need my medicine! Alice! I need it now!"

She must try again, and Alice flipped through the faded pages until she came to her favorite section. So romantic, so mysterious—Cairo, Alexandria, Mozambique, and Tangiers—holding the promise of heat and life. If she could only stay there long enough, consume enough to fill all those empty places inside…

She tore out the paragraph about Morocco: "*…in the open-air markets, you will find an incredible array of jewelry, leather, and brass, with shopkeepers eager to barter over prices…*" and slipped it between her teeth, letting it rest gently on her tongue. She could almost feel the heat and taste the sweet mint tea, almost hear the faint strange voices and the jangling of gold bracelets, almost touch the softness of the woolen rugs. Almost but not quite block out the noise from below.

If she lived there, she would wear a beautiful flowing *djellaba* with gold and silver threads running through the cloth. She could feel the weight of it against her skin, hear the sound it made as she walked amid the crowds of people. And all would bow reverently to her because she was someone special, someone of value and worth and respect.

"Alice!" Her mother's voice was too loud, too intrusive, able to reach all the way across the ocean. "My pills! I need my pills! Dammit to hell, where are you?"

More, she needed more—enough paper to build a boat, a plane, to construct wings to fasten on her body like Icarus, except she wouldn't fly too close to the sun but only close enough. She needed enough words to carry her far away, too far for that crazy, mean, needy old woman to follow.

She ripped an entire page from the atlas, stuffing the yellowed paper into her mouth, almost choking on the dryness—dry like the land, baked to hardness by the blazing sun. But the heat felt good, taking the coldness from her skin and bones and heart. She chewed faster, wanting to taste it all, absorb it all. To be *there*, to be anywhere but where she was right now in this minute, in this life.

"Alice!"

More pages. More words. More distance. "Cairo... Alexandria... Mozambique... Tangiers..."

The Sugar Bowl

Chloe would tell men that the slightly battered and tarnished sugar bowl was a legacy from her grandmother.

"Granny," she would say, her eyes fixed on a distant spot in the small apartment, "had to sell all her possessions to keep my mother fed and warm. But she saved the sugar bowl for better times. And when she died," here, her voice would quiver and a brave smile would slip across her face, "she left it for me, for my 'better times.'"

The story always worked on older men who brought her home after a pleasant dinner at an expensive restaurant. They would listen to her story as she poured the freshly-brewed coffee into delicate porcelain cups, her light brown hair falling softly around her face.

And they would be overcome with feelings of protectiveness for the young girl, so unlike the hard brittle career women they were used to. It would be almost obscene to think of taking this fragile flower to bed.

Instead they would kiss her chastely on the cheek and then leave, never understanding that it had all been carefully orchestrated—the dinner, the story, the quiver in the voice.

And if they should call again, Chloe would be politely unavailable. She could not support a return engagement. Her story was only strong enough for a single run.

Sometimes, on those Saturday nights when none of the men appealed to her or she didn't appeal to them, she'd return home and fix herself a steaming mug of cocoa, watching the heat rise in swirls across the dark brown surface.

Sipping the sweet liquid, she'd rehearse new versions of the sugar bowl story, trying in turn to look pensive or lonely or brave, or whatever emotion she thought would fit the tale and appeal to the men she brought home.

"This bowl?" she would ask, wide-eyed and smiling. "Why, this is from my Great-Granny, my grandmother's mum. She worked in one of those old English manor houses, and the master took such a fancy to her!"

"But, you know," and her voice would drop as she cast her eyes demurely to the ground, "it just wasn't done in those days to acknowledge a child born out of wedlock. Instead, she was sent away, although he did give her a silver tea set. It was worth a fortune. She sold it piece by piece, and the money she got for it saw her and the baby through the worst of the Depression. But she saved the sugar bowl to remember the sweetness of their love."

Or it was all that was left of the items stolen by her gypsy grandmother from the man who had left her "with child." Or, for those men attracted to bravery, it was the only item kept from the Nazis when they raided her great-grandparents' home.

"She kept it all those years," Chloe would whisper, "as a reminder of the cruel Germans who had shot her beloved husband to death while she, great with child, could do nothing to save him."

No one knew the truth of course. Sometimes even Chloe couldn't remember when she didn't have the sugar bowl.

If she had been an artist, she could have painted a likeness of those mythical women and no one, least of all Chloe, would have been able to tell that those features came not from memory but from her imagination.

She never tried to justify her stories to herself, but instead concentrated on developing new ones, adding to her repertoire as though, like Scheherazade, her very life depended on it.

She would enter those small upscale bars on the west side, choosing a man who looked as though he might be kind and understanding. Her purse would slip from her shoulder or her heel would catch on a nonexistent tear in the carpet, and the man would be at her side, offering assistance to the beautiful young girl who had been left waiting for a date who never came.

If no one was there, she would order a small glass of orange juice and sip it slowly until the glass was empty and it was time to return to the cold apartment filled with shadows of an imagined life.

Her stories were planned down to the last detail. They *couldn't* fail—had never failed Chloe in the past.

Each man was a mirror image of the last: hair turning gray and wrinkles at the corners of his eyes. He would be in his late fifties or so, the kind of man who would watch out for a young girl barely in her twenties. (Chloe was almost thirty-two in fact, but who could tell? Life had left no mark on her smooth, soft skin), He would be the kind of man she could safely bring home and trust to leave when she gave the almost imperceptible signal that the evening was over.

It had always worked before. But that night something went wrong. Was she tired and not as cautious as she usually was? Had the bar's dim lights deceived her? In any case, after dinner and a drink or two, the taxi ride to her apartment, and after she told her story, (Which one did she tell? She wasn't certain—they all seemed the same anymore) this man didn't leave. At least not until much later when it was too late for Chloe to cry out a new story.

If her door had not been left open, perhaps no one would have known what happened. But the sight of the bruised and battered figure lying there on the carpet just inside the room broke through the self-absorption of the neighbor passing by on her way to her own apartment. She called the police and then sat with Chloe until they arrived.

The female officer, skilled and professional, wrapped Chloe's shivering naked body in a blanket pulled from her disordered bed. But she couldn't break through the wall of silence Chloe had erected and resigned herself to a long wait for details.

Her partner, an older man yet still capable of being shocked by such casual cruelty, was moved to protectiveness by Chloe's vulnerable neck bowed in grief, her cold fingers tightly wrapped around a small silver object.

He reached over, gently touching her hand, and when Chloe released her grip, he took it from her.

"What a nice bowl," he said, and handed it back to Chloe, who turned her soft blue eyes toward him.

How gentle she is, he thought. *How could anyone harm her? She's so young, so delicate.*

Chloe saw his eyes grow tender and his hand reach out almost as though to stroke her cheek. An older man, she thought—a kind man who would feel sympathy for her because of all that she had suffered.

"This bowl?" she finally whispered, her voice scratchy and rough. "It belonged to my *arrière-grand-mère*, the mother of my grandmother, who was in the French Resistance during the war. She stole it from a man who had raped her and beat her and left her to die one cold winter night in a field just outside Paris. It is all I have left."

The Shop on the Square

The dirt road was bare and rutted. Bedraggled chickens scattered before the car's approach, the only sign of life in this isolated Mexican town.

The young man stopped the car and stepped out into the oppressive stillness. Heat and dust surrounded him, settling into the creases of his gray trousers, on his eyelashes and in his mouth. Everything tasted of the hot baking sun and the dry ground, and he had to swallow twice before his parched throat felt any relief.

Squinting in the brightness, he saw a shop nearby. The open doorway invited him to enter; the shadowed interior promising escape from the relentless sun. After carefully locking his car against intruders and thieves, he moved toward the darkness.

Inside the store, Mexican sombreros and brightly colored skirts hung on the walls, splayed out like three-dimensional paintings glowing against the whitewashed background. Everywhere he looked there were items for sale heaped on scarred wooden tables: stacks of garishly painted pottery and piles of serapes woven with the rays of dawn captured in their patterns.

But the dust from the street had invaded the shelves, dulling the bright colors. The store seemed to have few visitors—hardly surprising, he reflected, since he himself had stumbled across the town only because of several wrong turns during the long night of driving.

"What kind of people can live in a place like this?" he wondered aloud.

And as if in response, footsteps came from the silent darkness at the rear of the store: the shopkeeper coming to market her wares.

A small dark figure emerged: black eyes sparkling in a dark face, black skirt, blacker hair. The absence of colors should have depressed him but strangely it did not. The darkness reinforced the idea of coolness; bright colors meant heat, and he had had enough of that.

Absently, still staring at the woman, the young man picked up a wooden figure from a nearby table. At that, the proprietress smiled quickly at him, her white teeth a slash of brightness, and she quoted a figure that, even in Spanish, far exceeded the piece's value.

"No," he answered and quickly set the piece down again. He was too hot and too tired for a lengthy bargaining session in which he might understand only every other word. Besides, he hadn't come to buy anything except a few hours of respite from the sun.

"I didn't come to buy," he said in halting Spanish and shoved his hands into the pockets of his slacks as though to emphasize his words. "But I would like to rest. It is so hot, and I am tired. Have you a room I could sleep in for just a few American dollars?" He didn't want her to realize how desperately he needed to lie down and close his eyes against the sunlight.

She smiled again and then nodded eagerly, as though her greatest desire was to provide strangers with a place to sleep away the afternoon hours.

"*Siesta.*" With a sweep of her hand, she indicated an open doorway hung with a long striped blanket. "You sleep." The English words sounded unfamiliar when she spoke them.

Thank God, the young man thought, relieved as much by her understanding of his language as by her willingness to let him stay. After all, this place was a shop, not a hotel, and natives could be less than willing to offer hospitality to strangers.

Maybe it was because he looked exhausted. Or more likely, she must have seen his car, recognized him as a wealthy *Norte Americano*, and was determined to extract what money she could from his fortuitous arrival.

He pulled out his leather wallet, removing five ones from the stack neatly tucked inside. The shopkeeper's eyes gleamed, but she made no move to take the money. She just stood there patiently before him.

"Not enough?" he asked, a touch of irritation in his voice. What *was* the going-rate for a cheap bed in a dirt-poor Mexican village? Undoubtedly, it depended entirely on the desperation of the visitor. With a mental shrug, he pulled two more bills from the wad and then extended the money to the woman.

"For the room," he said, when she still made no move to take the money. "Surely this must be enough for a room for just a few hours."

But she only continued to smile in the dim light.

He shoved his wallet back into his pocket, hoping she'd understand that was all the money he was willing to offer. If she didn't agree, he would leave.

But the thought of tackling the desert in the heat of the day was almost more than he could accept.

If only I had stayed in the city overnight, he thought for the twentieth time. He could have resumed his journey in the cool morning hours and avoided getting lost in the darkness. He would never have ended up here in this godforsaken town, where a native intimidated him into offering three times the room's worth, just so he could escape the blazing sun and clinging dust that was Mexico.

"The room. Come see it." She pulled at his arm, her strength surprising him given her age. Or was it only that he was exhausted and lacked the energy to resist?

"But the money—"

Her eyes gleamed once more as she looked at the bills he held tightly in his hand.

"No pay now," she answered. "Later. When it is time. All visitors pay later." She turned, her gnarled hand still holding his arm, and moved toward the rear of the store.

Visitors? he wondered. *How many people came here? And why?*

He followed her through the doorway and around the corner to a small narrow room. He was so tired that he didn't care anymore what the room would cost. He'd pay anything just to lie down for a few hours in the cool darkness.

The room was dim, the closed shutters a shield against the blazing sunlight, and empty, save for a bed and a low chest against the white stucco wall.

"Sleep," she said, pointing to the bed. "*Siesta.*"

She turned down the starched white cotton sheet. "It has been many months since we had a visitor here. But the sheets, they are clean."

The young man looked longingly at the bed, but the woman continued to talk, seeming indifferent to his exhaustion. She moved around the room, straightening a cloth on top of the chest and brushing a speck of dirt from the face of the small statue on a corner shelf.

"Our *santo patrono*. Patron saint."

He dutifully looked at the painted plaster statue, poorly made and primitive in design, even for this backwater town.

"Today, we celebrate in his honor." She opened the shutters, letting in the full force of the sun's heat, and pointed out the window.

The young man squinted in the sudden blinding brightness. It was several seconds before he could make out the figures on a distant hillside—what appeared to be several boys leading a young calf down a stony path.

"For the feast," she said, and he understood that the calf was being brought in for slaughter. "It is tradition to kill a young calf to honor our saint," and she named one who was unfamiliar to him. One of the lesser-known ones, he guessed, remembered only by poor villagers who were not entitled to call upon the more popular saints for aid.

"You have this celebration every year?" he asked, more out of politeness than a genuine desire to know. But her answer surprised him.

"No, only when the saint provides for us. Sometimes he does not take good care of his people," and her eyes darkened with the memory. "Many grow sick, crops die, and there is no food to fill the empty bellies of our children. But sometimes," and the mournful look was gone, and her eyes sparkled like black diamonds, "the saint is good and sends us money—much money—and we can buy what we need."

Boy, the churches back home ought to hear about this one, the young man thought. He had heard of saints working miracles with health, but one who brings cold hard cash—well, that was a saint he could light a few candles to himself!

He grinned at the woman. "This money—does the saint bring it in checks or cash?"

But he saw instantly that he had caused offense. She turned her cold eyes upon him and muttered something under her breath, and even though the words were in Spanish, he understood enough to comprehend the need for an apology.

"I meant no disrespect," he said hastily, mentally tacking five more dollars onto the room's rent. He had better watch what he said. You never know with foreigners. "Perhaps you would let me come to the feast tonight," he added, relying on the charm that had never yet failed with clients or women. "That is, if you don't mind a foreigner at your table."

Her sudden spurt of laughter, over nearly as quickly as it started, disconcerted him. Then, she gazed at him gravely before replying. "Yes, I come for you when it is time. You will be our honored guest."

She latched closed the shutters then left the room, and it wasn't until the young man stretched out on the bed—dirty shoes carelessly soiling the white sheets, bulky wallet thrown on the low chest—that he considered her words.

Strange kind of feast day, he thought, *coming only at the whim of a saint.*

He turned his sweaty face against the lace-trimmed pillow, his thoughts wandering. *When people are this poor, I suppose they must take their joy where they can find it. Decent of her to let me to come tonight.*

He smothered a yawn and shut his eyes, glad she had pulled the shutters closed.

Poor people always seemed more generous than the rich was his final drowsy thought. *Perhaps that is why they are poor*—and on that reflection, he fell asleep.

Hours later he awoke, unsure of the time. The air in the room was hot and stale, and when he opened the shutters in the hope of a cool breeze, he saw the setting sun.

Looking at his watch, he realized it was far later than he had thought. The woman must have decided to let him sleep until the feast was underway. For the first time since she had told him about the celebration, he wondered at the source of the money allegedly brought by the saint.

Surely, the woman's meager rental charge would be hardly enough for a party. Could it a legacy from a villager who had traveled far from this miserable town to make his fortune?

It couldn't be from a sudden surge in the tourist trade, remembering the layer of dust covering the items in the store. The place looked as if it had been undisturbed for quite a while. So where did the money come from?

His mind turned the problem over. The old woman wasn't even eager to take his money, he realized. "Later," she had said, and suddenly he remembered his wallet, which he had carelessly tossed onto the chest near the door. He had been so tired that he could have slept through an army invading his room, let alone one small woman who had seen how many dollars he had tucked inside.

Rapidly, he crossed the room and picked up his wallet. But when he opened it, he saw that not one bill was missing.

His face flushed with shame, and he was conscious of having done the old woman a disservice. She had given him a bed and invited him to the village celebration—what kind of cynical man had he become to believe she would have stolen his money? These were simple folk with a code of honor that was long forgotten in the north.

The noise from outside drew him back to the window. Shading his eyes, he saw, next to the shop, a small open space crowded with villagers. Rough tables and benches had been set up, and the aroma of roasting beef drifted tantalizingly his way.

"Poor calf," he said. "You're the guest of honor at the party, and you can't even enjoy the feast."

"Guest of honor"—where had he heard that phrase?

He was still puzzling over the question, absentmindedly turning his wallet over and over in his hands, when he heard a knock at the door.

"Come in," he called, and suddenly he remembered what the shopkeeper had said earlier. "Honored guest," she had called him, and this saint—

this strange patron saint of the village—who brings money, real money, the kind of money that was in his wallet, growing heavier by the second.

"Come in," he called again, his voice trembling, and he clenched his expensive leather wallet filled with American currency—enough to keep a small town well-fed for several months—with fingers suddenly grown cold.

Reason enough for a celebration, he thought crazily.

The old woman stood in the doorway, her dark hair and clothes indistinguishable in the shadows. She moved into the room, and the last fading rays of the sun were reflected in her eyes and glittered on the long blade of the carving knife she held in her hand.

"Come, honored guest," she said softly, and he could almost swear there was a touch of pity in her voice.

She would speak that way, he thought inconsequentially, to the poor calf as she drew him closer for the slaughter.

"Come," she said again. "It is time."

Watching for Billy

The chime of the security alarm woke Agnes from her usual afternoon nap. One of the curses of old age was the need to nap at odd hours of the day, coupled with the inability to stay asleep at night. And since Roger died, it was even worse. Agnes found herself nodding off at midmorning while watching the game shows, during the afternoon courtroom dramas, after her soup and sandwich dinner that was her evening meal. But why not? There was no one to talk to and nothing else to do.

Her son Brad said that she wouldn't be bored if she would move into a retirement home. But she didn't want to leave her house and live with strangers even if the loneliness was sometimes more than she could bear.

"I've lived here more than sixty years, and I'm not leaving now," she had told him. "There's nothing you can say that will change my mind."

"Fine," he answered with the familiar note of irritation in his voice. "But if you won't move, you need to at least have an alarm installed. There have been too many break-ins in your neighborhood lately."

Agnes reluctantly agreed. She supposed her son meant well, although she wondered if it wasn't more for his own peace of mind than her safety. It wasn't worth arguing about though. And he was right about the old neighborhood. It had slowly deteriorated as longtime friends and neighbors died or moved to the suburbs, their once pristine houses chopped up into cheap apartments that drew the worst elements like maggots to rotting meat.

So, she had let Brad have his way and she was dutifully attentive when the technician explained how the alarm worked and what each noise and light represented.

"You'll hear a chime if a door or window is opened, even if the alarm isn't on," he had told her. "But if the alarm is set, the siren will sound. And here" and he pointed to the part of the panel where tiny lights glowed, "these lights will show you where the problem is: green for closed and red for open."

During the long summer days, she didn't bother to activate the system until bedtime, trusting the safety of daylight to keep thieves and robbers away from her door. But as winter drew near, she found herself turning on the alarm at the first sign of dusk, feeling for the first time a little unsure, a little vulnerable, in the house where she had lived for six decades.

The alarm—she'd better see what the problem was. Hurrying to the back entry where the control panel was mounted, she squinted at the touchpad. A steady red light indicated that there was something amiss, and putting on her bifocals, she was able to make out the source of the trouble. According to the indicator, the cellar door was open.

"When the alarm sounds, don't investigate. Call the police," the technician had warned her, but Agnes had no intention of disrupting her neighbors with flashing lights and wailing sirens. She had probably failed to shut the door tightly enough when she took the garbage out and the November wind had blown it back open. It would be a simple task to go to the landing and see if that was the problem.

Turning on the light switch, she could tell that the door at the foot of the steps was indeed ajar, just enough to set off the alarm. But what she hadn't expected to see was a line of wet footprints leading from the doorway across the cement. And there were rustling sounds, too. Someone was down there—someone was in her house!

Her heart started pounding in the quick way it did when she was frightened or upset, the familiar angina clutching at her chest in response to the increased tempo. She turned to—what? Call for help? No one could hear her.

A figure detached itself from the shadows to stand at the foot of the stairs. "Don't worry. I won't hurt you."

The voice was that of a young boy—barely in his teens, she judged. When he moved more into the light, she saw his tousled brown hair and dirty face, his thin shoulders barely covered by the torn dark blue jacket he wore—far too lightweight to protect him from the wind.

"I was cold and hungry, and then I saw that the door was open. I thought maybe I could get something to eat and sleep for a bit before I had to go back out there." He gestured to the outside, where a steady icy rain had started to fall.

The sound of the rain, as much as the plaintive tone in his voice, decided her. She knew that she ought to call the authorities or, at the very least, demand that he leave. The newspapers were full of stories about elderly people being attacked in their homes by intruders. Wasn't that the reason—or one of the reasons, anyway—why Brad wanted her to sell the house and move into a nursing home?

But she trusted in her mother's instincts to tell a good child from a bad. Besides, she was all alone and dinnertime was fast approaching. What harm could it do to feed him before sending him on his way? And maybe give him one of Roger's jackets, one of the few that she hadn't given away after his funeral.

"What's your name?"

"Billy," he answered, moving onto the bottom step.

"Hello, Billy. My name is Agnes. Why don't you come upstairs and have something to eat?" she asked.

The boy moved quickly, as though he wasn't surprised at her decision, as though he had known all along what she would say.

Agnes made spaghetti, apologizing for the lack of meatballs. "I don't cook much these days," she said, ladling store-brand sauce over the angel hair pasta Roger had loved. "When my husband was alive, everything I cooked was homemade and he ate it all, not even leaving enough for leftovers. But since he died, well, there isn't much point in cooking for one, is there?"

The boy wiped the sauce from his plate with a slice of white bread and drank all his milk before looking at her.

"No family?" he asked.

"My son Brad lives too far to visit except for the holidays. Roger and I only had the one child, you see, and Brad never married, so there aren't any grandchildren." Unexpectedly, the tears came. It had been a long time since she had cried.

"I'm sorry," she whispered, wiping her eyes and blowing her nose. She gathered up their plates. "It's just that I get lonesome sometimes. But enough about me. Where do you live? Where are your parents?"

It might've been a story from a Dickens novel: abused child runs away from home with no one to take him in other than even more abusive foster parents, reduced to living by his wits: begging, stealing, and lying just to survive. He recounted his story with no trace of self-pity as though it was something he had read somewhere and retold just for her.

"You know, it isn't that hard to get into houses. People leave doors unlocked, or they hide the key in a place that anybody could think of," Billy explained. "I can always tell when people are gone on a trip, too. They don't take their trash cans out on garbage day, or newspapers would be blowing all over the yard. No one has ever caught me," he boasted, twisting in his seat to look around the room.

She knew she ought to tell him that such behavior was wrong, and then call the police, or at least send him away. But it was so dark outside. And the house seemed less lonely with another person in it.

"Would you like to stay here?" she asked. "For the night, I mean."

He looked around again as though judging the value of the offer and then nodded his head. He rose from his chair. "I'll just lock the cellar door so no one else comes in. Okay?"

It didn't take Agnes long to wash the few dishes, and while she worked, she was conscious of him drifting around inside the house. Once she was done, she joined Billy in the living room, taking her seat in the rocking chair by the window while he continued to move around the room. He picked up a high school photo of Brad, looked at it critically, and then put it back. He fingered the television remote and then moved on to the radio sitting on the end table. Once or twice, she thought he was on the verge of opening a drawer or checking inside a cabinet, but surely she was wrong. He was just bored, killing time until bed. That's all.

"Would you like to do something?" she said, getting up from her chair. She realized she was uncomfortable with the way he seemed to be prowling around the room. "Or perhaps you're tired and you'd rather go to sleep."

"Not me! Not yet anyway," he said, coming over to stand by her, almost too close. She stepped back a bit but then, embarrassed by her instinctive recoil, put her hand on the back of the chair as if she just needed to steady herself. She didn't want him to think she didn't trust him. Of course she did. He was just a lost, abandoned child after all who needed somebody to take care of him.

"Well, then," she said, and casting about for something to do, she caught sight of the domino game on the bookshelf. "Do you know how to play dominos, Billy? My husband Roger and I used to play every Sunday evening—" She stopped, her throat suddenly full of grief.

Billy glanced quickly up at her and then crossed the room to retrieve the game from the shelf. "Come on, then," he said leading the way to the dining room table. "Let's play."

The rest of the evening passed enjoyably, even though Billy turned out to be an adept domino player, winning game after game until the clock chimed eleven. A few times, she wondered if he were cheating. Or maybe it was her fault. Her sight was not as good as it used to be and it was difficult for her to make out the number of tiny black dots even against the ivory background. But although Billy couldn't help but notice how closely she peered at each one, he never volunteered to tell her how many were there.

Or perhaps she was being unfair. After all, he was young. How was he supposed to know what it was like to be old, how the sight failed until it was almost impossible to tell exactly what one was looking at?

"I won again," Billy announced, but with no trace of victory in his voice. How different from Roger, Agnes thought, who would take an almost childish glee in beating her game after game. But she didn't mind losing. She wasn't playing to win, just for company.

"Yes, you did," Agnes agreed, adding up her numbers before pushing the tiles into one large pile. "Now why don't you help me put these away and then we can have something to eat before bed—some cocoa and cookies, I think. Would you like that, Billy?"

He looked at her with a gaze that was hard to identify before smiling. "Yes, cocoa and cookies would be nice," almost, but not quite, mocking her.

Yet it *was* nice, the two of them sitting on the sofa, munching slightly stale cookies and sipping cocoa made from packets. So nice, in fact, that she was disappointed when he took his mug into the kitchen. Billy, it seemed, was done with his bedtime snack and if she didn't hurry, he might change his mind and leave her.

Agnes gulped the rest of the hot liquid, burning her throat in the process, before pushing to her feet. "I'll show you to your room," sounding like an over-anxious hostess who was afraid her guests would leave before the party was over. "Just let me check the doors—"

"And set the alarm," Billy added with a slight laugh.

She glanced at him quickly, not certain if he was making fun of her, but decided it was just a harmless tease. "Yes. And set the alarm," moving to the panel where she tapped in the code: four zeroes, simple enough to remember.

Once upstairs, she led the way to Brad's old bedroom. "You can sleep here. I'll get you a pair of my husband's pajamas to wear. They'll be large, but at least you'll be warm."

"The bathroom is down the hall," she added, pointing in the direction away from the staircase, "and my room is that way, just before the steps. If you need anything, just call me."

"Don't worry, I'll manage," Billy answered. "And thanks so much for letting me stay. You know, most people wouldn't let a stranger, even a kid, stay in their home like this. You really should be more careful."

Agnes shook her head and smiled. "That's what my son keeps telling me. But I like to think I'm a good judge of people. You seem like a nice boy who has just had some bad breaks. What you need is someone to look after you and keep you from going in the wrong direction."

"Yes," he said thoughtfully. "I guess I do need someone to watch me." He gently closed his door.

Later that night, Agnes awoke to the sound of footsteps passing her door. She thought at first that Billy had forgotten the way to the bathroom, but when she heard the creak of the step (the third one from the bottom) she knew he had gone downstairs.

She pushed herself up from the bed and, pulling on her old terrycloth robe, followed him. Perhaps he felt guilty about trespassing on her kindness and wanted to leave without making a fuss. Whatever he planned, she had to stop him. He was too young and vulnerable to live alone by his wits. She was older—she could protect him, give him what he needed.

But when she turned on the kitchen light, she found that what he needed—or wanted—wasn't someone to protect him, unless he thought that someone was to be found in her silver chest. His hands were full of knives, forks, spoons—tarnished wedding presents from more than a half century ago.

"Billy?"

He looked up at her, no trace of guilt or remorse on his face. "I'm sorry. Did I wake you?"

There was no doubt in her mind that he planned to steal the items. And while she realized that she knew nothing about the boy—nothing except what he told her—she was suddenly too tired to cope with the disappointment. Tomorrow she would have a talk with him, the kind of talks she used to have with Brad when she caught him doing something wrong. Then he would understand and they could have a pleasant day together.

"Put the silverware back and go to bed, Billy. We'll talk about it in the morning," her tone the same as when she would chastise Brad about some minor infraction.

Billy carefully set the pieces down in their appointed slots and then closed the chest and took it back to the dining room.

"You know, you really ought to polish those," he remarked as he passed her on his way up the stairs. "They're nice pieces, but they need to be cleaned."

Agnes watched him go, feeling a trace of foreboding. Perhaps she had been too quick to give him a place to sleep. After all, she really *didn't* know anything about him. And the papers were full of stories about old people murdered in their beds by kids on drugs, looking for fast cash to feed their growing habit.

"But Billy *isn't* on drugs," she said to herself, slowly climbing the stairs. "I would know, I'm sure. *Any* mother would know these things."

The next morning, Agnes came downstairs to a veritable feast: scrambled eggs, toast spread with butter and jelly, and even fresh-perked coffee—a treat she no longer allowed herself since Roger died. A pot of coffee was a waste, she had decided, since she drank only one cup a day.

"I hope you don't mind," Billy said, smiling at her.

She smoothed her hair and pulled the sash of her old robe a little tighter—the age-old feminine reaction to the presence of a male. And if, in some corner of her mind, she realized that the incident with the silver was not going to be addressed, she let it go. That was then, and this was now. Perhaps this meal was Billy's way of apologizing for abusing her trust.

"Thank you." She sat down while he poured her some coffee and set the sugar bowl and creamer within her reach. "Aren't you eating?"

"I already helped myself," he answered, watching her. "I thought I'd go to the store and get a few things—that was the last of the eggs, you know. And maybe sweep the sidewalk. The leaves can be slippery. I wouldn't want you to fall."

She stirred her coffee, blinking back tears. It had been a long time since someone had looked after her. Once Roger had his stroke, he couldn't take care of himself, let alone do anything for her.

She blew her nose before answering. "Thank you, Billy. Let me finish this wonderful breakfast you made for me and then I'll get you some money for the store."

"Oh, don't worry." He slipped on his jacket—or was it Roger's? She couldn't tell without her glasses. "I have what I need." With that, he was gone.

In his absence, the breakfast lost its flavor. Agnes took only a few more bites of her toast before carrying her dish to the sink. Was this what she had come to— needing someone in her house to make meals worth eating, life worth living again?

Slipping on her coat, she walked out onto the small back porch to throw what was left of her bread out for the birds. It wasn't until she came back in that she realized the alarm hadn't sounded. Surely, she had set it last night before they had gone upstairs. She remembered Billy teasing her about it.

Or had she forgotten to do it, distracted by having someone in the house? And if it *had* been on, then who had disarmed it?

"I did," Billy explained later when he returned. "I was going in and out, taking out the trash and stuff, and I was afraid that it would wake you up."

If Agnes was surprised that he had somehow guessed the code, she didn't let on. But for the rest of the day, as she watched Billy move around the house—first upstairs, then down, into the basement and then back up again—she was torn between a sense of unease that something was wrong and a fear that he might walk right out the door and leave her alone.

That night, when she heard the footsteps on the stairs, she turned away from the sound. She didn't want to know what he was doing; she didn't want to confront him. She was afraid of what he might do. Or was she was afraid he might leave?

The next morning followed the same pattern as the day before, except that Agnes changed out of her nightgown and into her Sunday dress before coming downstairs. The least she could do, she decided, was dress up since she had company.

Once again, Billy had made breakfast—pancakes, this time, topped with blueberry sauce—and hot coffee. Instant though, she noticed and wondered why. But she didn't want to ask. She would sound ungrateful, especially since he had made such a nice meal.

They ate the meal together, and then Billy went out. To do what? Agnes wondered but let it go. Instead, she kept herself busy, putting beef bones on to boil to make soup before rummaging through boxes in the attic to find some of Brad's clothes that might fit the young boy. And later that night, after a dinner of meatloaf, canned corn, and applesauce, she and Billy played dominos again.

"You watch too much television," he had said half teasingly when she had reached for the remote. "And there's nothing good on anyway—just a lot of stories about crime. Come on, it's time for our game."

Obediently, Agnes set the remote down and took her place at the dining room table where he had set out the tiles. It wasn't until the next day, when the time came for the Judge Ruth Jones show, that she realized the television wasn't working. No matter which button she pushed on the remote, the screen remained blank and unresponsive.

"Billy?" she called, waiting for him to answer from the basement. He had said he was looking for a screwdriver—why, she didn't know. But it didn't matter. He was quite handy and no doubt, something needed fixing. Something *always* needed fixing in this old house, and she didn't have the knowledge or energy to take care of them.

"What's up?"

She was startled. She hadn't heard him approaching. She handed him the remote and gestured toward the screen. "It won't work," sounding like a little child with a broken toy. "I tried and tried, but it won't turn on."

Billy fiddled around behind the television set for a bit and then frowned.

"I think the power supply is shorting out," he said, not quite looking at her. He unplugged the television and carried it to the back door, and then set the remote control on top of it.

"I'll take it to someone who can fix it. Okay?" Without waiting for her answer, he slipped on his coat, propped open the door, and carried the television outside, returning a minute later to carefully close the door behind him.

Agnes chose not to ask where he was taking her television or why the remote had seemed unusually light in her hand—almost as though the batteries were missing.

Instead, she went to the freezer and took out a package of chicken pieces. "I'll make breaded chicken for dinner," she said aloud. "And some mashed potatoes," although she would have to mash them by hand. The stand mixer she had had for years was missing, as was the percolator—the one Billy had used just the other morning.

That night, Billy again won all the domino games, in part because Agnes was too preoccupied to pay attention.

"Is something wrong?" he asked, while he returned the tiles to their box. "You're not talking as much as usual tonight." The look of concern on his face warmed her heart and almost stopped her from what she was going to say.

But a mother must look out for her young, she told herself. "No, Billy, there's nothing wrong. But I think we need to talk about your future," she said. "I mean, you can't stay here forever, you know. Someone will be looking for you, and I could get into a lot of trouble by keeping you here without permission."

He closed the dominos box and set it on the shelf, right where the silverware chest used to be.

"Billy?"

"Let's talk about this in the morning," he said finally. "We'll get it all straightened out then."

"My son is coming tomorrow," she said, surprising herself. It wasn't like her to tell falsehoods but somehow, she felt it was important for him to know she wasn't alone even though Brad hadn't come to see her in months. "We'll need to explain it to him."

"Go to bed, Agnes," Billy said gently, and, turning her toward the steps, he gave her a slight push, the way a parent might send a recalcitrant child off to sleep.

When Agnes awoke the next morning, there was an unaccustomed quiet to the house. No noises from the kitchen, no aroma of breakfast wafting up the stairs—and when she came downstairs, she found the house deserted.

Billy was gone. *And* the grocery money she kept in the kitchen drawer *and* the silver tea set she and Roger had received from Brad on their twenty-fifth wedding anniversary *and* the mantel clock Roger had brought from England when he came back from the war. Even the domino set was gone, although she couldn't imagine it had much value on the street.

It was all gone. She was left with nothing, no one.

Agnes walked to the back door and looked out, watching, watching, even though there was nothing, no one, to see—even though she didn't really expect to see Billy.

"Billy?" she called. And then louder, "Billy?"

But no one answered.

She shut and locked the door, and then walked over to the alarm panel. Four zeroes and the alarm was set.

She knew she ought to call the police, report the theft, and provide them with a description of the young boy. Or, at the very least, she ought to call her son, tell him how foolish she had become in her old age, agree that a nursing home *would* be the best place for her before something really bad happened.

Instead, she put on some water to boil for instant coffee And when she couldn't find the toaster, she settled for butter on a slice of cold bread.

And then sat down to watch for Billy.

The Healer

"Just let me touch you. Please—just one touch. The tip of my finger, then. Please, can I touch you with the tip of my finger? Please? Just for a second. Please!"

Begging. Pleading. The voice of desperation. Cassie had heard it so many times before and, in the beginning, in the early days, had found it impossible to ignore. So she would stand there, let them touch her, stroke her face, cut tiny pieces of faded cloth from her shirt, her jeans—once, even a strand of hair from her head, done so quickly that she couldn't shield her scalp from the sharp blade of the scissors. And with each touch, she felt more of herself being taken, being lost.

But today, she turned a deaf ear to the words, hardened her heart to the emotion behind the plea. She had to. Otherwise, there would be nothing of her left at the end of the day. She would be in a million separate pieces, scattered to the four corners of the world, a disembodied force forever longing for a body into which it could once again reside.

Cassie was a healer. At least, that was what the people who touched her said. *She* never touched anyone though. She just stood there while they approached, hardly daring to breathe for fear they would find a way to take away even the breath from her body. Then, with one or two trembling fingers, these people—these needy, needy people—would tentatively reach out and lightly caress the sleeve of her jacket, the back of her neck, her forehead where every day, new wrinkles scarred their way across the thin skin.

Every time they touched her, Cassie would shiver, as though, molecule by molecule, life-giving heat was being drained from her. But then it passed (and it always passed) and she would be warm again—maybe not as warm as she would like to be but then, as her Granny had always reminded her when she complained of the cold, drained feeling that followed a touching, "You have a gift. But a gift comes with a cost. That's just the way it is, Cassandra, and you'd better get used to it."

She ought to be used to it by now. People had been touching her for twenty years, since she was just a child of eight—the first time she had done a healing, the first time, in fact, that she knew she possessed such a strange power. A woman had handed her a cat—a dirty white mass of fleas and fur and bones—begging her to "please fix it! She won't eat or drink. And my kids are beside themselves! She can't die!"

The mother looked as half-starved as the animal, her eyes wild with misery, pain, and fear. Cassie didn't know what to do. She had never done a healing before, although often enough she had watched her grandmother work her touch on the old, infirm, damaged dregs of humanity who would cross the threshold of their secluded farmhouse.

She never understood how these strangers had found her grandmother. The two of them lived far from town, down a rutted dirt road that was muddy in the spring, hard and rocky in the summer, and dangerously icy when winter whistled its way through the mountains.

But find her they did, and now, they were finding Cassie as well, hoping against hope that the gift had passed from grandparent to grandchild—the gift that couldn't save her mother who had died giving Cassie life.

Cassie used to wonder if she was not, in some way, responsible for her mother's death. Had she greedily inhaled her mother's breath into her own fragile lungs? Had her birth drained her mother of life? Or was she her mother's final healing? By taking the gift from her mother into her own tiny body, had Cassie freed her mother from the draining existence that her life had become?

Her mother hated being a healer. Cassie knew that, had heard her grandmother say it often enough.

"She fought it—with every bit of her being, she fought against the gift. When she laid with that man"—"that man" was how Cassie's grandmother referred to the person who had co-created Cassie— "she thought it would free her from it. 'I just want to be normal, Mama,' she used to cry. But I told her that, for her, this *was* normal; this was the way it had to be. And she had to accept it."

But she never did. And now it was Cassie's turn to either accept or forever fight against what she had not asked for—a future she could never avoid.

That cat—Cassie remembered how it looked wearily at her, mutely asking for death before closing its eyes. She had touched it, brushing the fleas from the scabby skin, running her fingers across the head and down the back until she reached its tail. The animal gave one convulsive gasp and then went limp in her arms and, for a moment, she was certain that she had killed it. But then, the tail began to twitch, ever so weakly, like a tree branch responding to a gentle breeze, and she heard the telltale hum that vibrated from its throat. The cat was purring. She had handed it back to the woman and then turned, shivering, to go into the house.

That was the beginning of Cassie's life as a healer—and the end of her life as a normal child. Not that she did a healing every day—sometimes weeks would go by before anyone approached her, asking her for help, begging her to heal their sick pet, their ill child, their dying parent.

Sometimes the healing didn't work and the people would leave as hurt as they arrived, although oddly enough, they didn't hold her responsible for the failure. Perhaps they thought the gods who had granted her the gift of healing had judged them unworthy of its use. Cassie didn't ask. But when a healing failed, she couldn't help feeling that somehow it *was* her fault that they couldn't get what they wanted.

"But then who does?" asked her grandmother unsympathetically when Cassie would broach the subject. "Who on this earth gets what they want every time they ask for it? No one does. Anyone who says they do is a liar and anyone who thinks they will is a fool."

Cassie used to wonder how someone so devoid of sympathy, empathy, or genuine caring could be a healer. But that was in the early days, before she knew what a toll the healings would take on her. As more and more bits of her disappeared, she saw the need to put up a wall between herself and the people who wanted something from her that she did not want to give.

She hated her gift. She never wanted it and couldn't understand what evil she had done to be cursed with such a talent. "I just want to be like everyone else!" she had cried late one night after a particularly draining healing.

But her grandmother only shrugged her bony shoulders. "You are as you are, Cassandra. You can't change what you have or what you can do. Don't fight it. Just accept it."

No sympathy there—no pity for the bewildered child who was expected to fix conditions beyond her understanding, no comfort for the adolescent who wanted to be like everyone else her age, worrying about school and boyfriends and clothes, even though Cassie's concerns rose far above those teenage anxieties. Each day she worried that someone would come with that begging desperate look in their eyes. Each time, she worried that this healing would be her last, that it would drain her of life once and for all.

And now, since her grandmother was gone, she had no one to talk to, no one who understood. All she could do was hope that the world would forget about Cassie-the-Healer and let her live what was left of this life.

"My neighbor told me you helped her. Please. Can't I just touch you?"

The woman in front of her (And why were there so many more women than men who came to her for help?) was well dressed, her shoes unscuffed, the rings on her manicured fingers sparkling in the sunlight. Yet the look in her eyes was the same as all the other fearful frightened people.

Cassie remembered her. She had seen her in the store last week when she was buying her milk and bread, had noticed her in the congregation the few times she attended church, and had recognized the familiar expression of desperation, anger, and fear that characterized those who visited her.

Once, she had come within three feet of Cassie, who waited there with the hopelessness of a trapped animal to see what would happen, what she wanted, how much she would take. But then the woman had turned and walked away, and Cassie breathed again. There was something about her, something about that woman that Cassie feared, more than she feared the gift itself.

"I need help. You have to help me! I've waited so long to speak to you, touch you. Please, can I touch you?"

This was a woman who could pay for medical care for whatever problem was plaguing her. So why did she come to Cassie?

For a moment, Cassie considered letting it happen—a healing or not, but certainly a draining. But it had been a long, hard month and she had nothing left, no reserves that would keep her alive should she allow one more person to touch her. Ever since she buried her grandmother four weeks ago, she had been running on empty.

A simple graveside service, the words "We are dust and unto dust we shall return," the sound of the dirt falling on the coffin top like sleet—and Cassie left standing there alone.

"I can't help you," she said to the woman before turning to walk away, conscious of the pervasive weakness that dogged her waking hours. Every day it was a little harder to move through life, her gift a growing weight on her shoulders. She wished it would go away. Or that she could go away.

But the woman blocked her path, saying all the while, "You have to! You have to help me! I need it! You have to!" her voice rising in volume.

Cassie looked at the wild-eyed, desperate woman and saw danger in her face, heard it in her voice, felt it emanating from her body like a treacherously cold chill.

Something was wrong here. If she healed this woman—if she let her touch her even for a moment—Cassie feared there would be nothing left of her. She would die as surely as her grandmother did, as her mother did—her life force sucked from her fragile body by someone who rated her own need for help as more important than Cassie's need to live.

"I can't go on! I can't bear it anymore! You have to help me!" all the while coming closer to Cassie until it seemed she was sucking in Cassie's every exhalation. "You've helped other people—I know because I asked and they said you were a healer. What right do you have to refuse me? I can pay! I have money! But you have to heal me!" insistent, as though by the force of her words she could make the healing energy slip from Cassie's body into hers.

"Let me pass!" Cassie tried to escape, but she was no match for the desperation that drove the woman.

"I can't heal you! I can't! You don't understand! I'll die if I heal you!"—the last a cry from Cassie's heart that, as she voiced it, she knew to be true. One more healing and she *would* die. Too many years, too much drained from her, with nothing going back into that well that was her soul.

"You'll die if you don't!"

Cassie saw it then, the thin flashing blade wielded by those manicured, beringed fingers, the hand that came even closer to her. "You *will* heal me! I tell you, you will! I came all this way and you can't say no to me! I demand a healing! Now!"

Cassie stood there, mutely shaking her head. She couldn't—she just couldn't.

The blade was quite sharp—it must have been to slice so quickly and cleanly through the faded white t-shirt Cassie wore, through her skin, her muscles, into her heart. In the end, it was even sharp enough to cut the ties that kept her gift bound to her. Cassie felt it leaving her with each spurt of blood that pumped onto the grass where she lay.

"There! Now heal yourself!" and the woman vanished from sight. Or was she still there, but invisible in the growing darkness that obscured Cassie's vision?

This must be how a healing feels, thought Cassie. First a shock, almost a pain, but not quite—more like an electrical current jolting through her body, mind, soul. Then a lightness, a sense of buoyancy, weightlessness—the burden of her gift no longer pulling at her, dragging at her.

All her energy was running full blast like fire through her veins. Cassie didn't know when she had ever felt so alive, so light. With each drop of blood that stained the earth, with each pulse of her heart, slowing down, beat by infinitesimal beat, Cassie felt herself losing the terrible gift that had drained her for so many years.

She breathed in the healing, drank it like a thirsting man gulps down cool, fresh water, wrapped it around her like a blanket on a cold winter night, until darkness came and she was finally free, finally healed.

The Clock

"Harold," said Margaret, sneaking up behind him and startling him so he lost his place in the Sunday crossword, "how many times do I have to tell you to wind the clock? Do I have to do *all* your thinking for you?"

"*Harold!*" rapping the top of his head where his gray hair had thinned to expose vulnerable pink flesh. "Are you listening to me? Wind the clock!"

Harold stirred his seventy-five-year-old body from the safe depths of his easy chair and headed toward the offending timepiece. There would be no rest until the clock was wound and set ticking again.

"Yes, Margaret, I'll wind the clock. Although," he ventured, rummaging in the side drawer for the key, "I really think it should be repaired. It never seems to stay running very long."

"'You think,' 'you think,'" mimicked Margaret, her words tiny thorns unaccompanied by roses. After fifty-five years together, Harold had stopped searching for flowers. "You're just too lazy to wind it! You don't do anything else and now you even want to pay somebody to do this for you!"

Harold climbed onto the low footstool to reach the clock, trying with limited success to ignore her. He had learned long ago not to argue but just to let her words engulf him. So far, they had always stopped short of drowning him, although sometimes it was awfully close. Then, when her tirade would finally subside, he would have to go outside for a breath of fresh air.

"The least you could do around here is drag your useless body out of that damn chair and wind the clock when it runs down!"

I wish *you'd* run down, you old bitch, thought Harold, and then was surprised at the sudden, almost overwhelming hatred that ran through him like lifeblood.

Reaching up, he carefully inserted the small brass key into the clock face. As he turned it slowly and methodically, he pictured his wife winding down— her words coming slower and slower until she stopped altogether and he was granted the welcome absence of sound.

"Harold, are you *done* yet? Why does it always take you so long to finish every little job?" Margaret's voice lashed Harold, jerking him back to reality as his daydream faded. She came up beside him to peer shortsightedly at the clock, which hadn't yet begun to run.

"Are you winding it right, Harold?" jabbing him in the side to catch his attention. "You know you have to turn the key clockwise or it will stop again." And she poked him once more for emphasis.

Harold winced. He wished she wouldn't keep hitting him there. After all these years, his side had become very tender.

He removed the key from the clock and gently tapped the pendulum, setting the small brass circle swaying. With luck, the clock would continue to run, forcing Margaret to spend several silent minutes finding something else to complain about and gaining him a brief measure of much-needed quiet.

Harold slipped the key back into the cluttered drawer and resumed his seat in the easy chair, determined to finish the puzzle before Margaret used the paper to wrap garbage. Sometimes she would seize it just when he was almost through and dump coffee grounds across the neatly filled-in blocks, obliterating what small victories he had achieved.

But peace, so long awaited, lasted only until he picked up his pencil. Then the clock stopped.

"There, Harold," gloated Margaret. "I told you to be careful and now listen! The clock has stopped again! I can't even depend on you to wind a clock right!"

Her words prodded him from his chair and toward the clock once more. He touched the pendulum hopefully, but it refused to maintain an even arc of motion, only swaying a bit before stopping altogether.

And all the while, Margaret's voice relentlessly attacked his unprotected back, letting loose a volley of poison-tipped verbal darts that would kill a less experienced man.

"You're good for nothing, Harold! I've known that for years! To think I've wasted my whole life with someone as useless as you!"

Perhaps a screwdriver would loosen it… Harold reached back into the side drawer, pushing aside the key that had been no help at all, and found the thin-bladed tool. He climbed awkwardly back onto the stool, holding the screwdriver tightly in his clenched fist.

"What do you think you're going to do with that, Mr. Fix-It? You think you can make it work now? Haven't you done enough damage for one day?"

Harold inserted the metal edge into the narrow opening. Maybe if he turned it just a bit, the clock would start and Margaret would stop, at least for awhile.

She came up beside him, her words flooding from her as though from a broken dam.

"Harold, leave it *alone* already! You don't know what you're doing anyway! I don't know why I talk to you, you stupid old man!"

Her words spilled over his ankles. The tide was rising and Harold knew from experience it would flow higher yet. He slowly turned the screwdriver as Margaret continued, although he was finding it harder to breathe against the weight of her words, now reaching his chest.

"Damn it, Harold, turn it the *other* way! You're doing it wrong!" And now the tide was higher and stronger than it had ever been before. Harold had to stop for a moment to catch his breath before trying once more to wind the clock.

"Are you *deaf*, Harold? I told you a thousand times already! Turn it clockwise or it will stop again!"

Harold plunged the screwdriver in as far as it would go, carefully turning it counter-clockwise until the handle was too slippery to grasp.

Then, he lightly stepped off the stool, breathing easier in the silence.

"You're right, Margaret," he remarked, looking down at the crumpled figure. "It did stop."

Anything Can Happen

"Where *are* my keys?"

Charlotte *always* put them on the hook right by the front door. It was the same procedure she followed each night when she came home from work.

First, before she'd even go inside, she'd check to make sure the door was locked, that she *had* bolted it securely against any intruders when she had left that morning. Then she would unlock all three bolts, slip inside, and quickly lock them behind her, before hanging her key ring on the small brass hook next to the doorframe.

Only then would she set her handbag on the side table and hang up her coat, before looking around to make sure everything was where it should be.

Sometimes, if the day had been particularly stressful, she would even go back and double-check, just to make sure the door really was locked and the keys were where they belonged, that they hadn't somehow disappeared from their appointed location.

And yet, this morning, the hook was empty. No key ring hanging there. No keys on the floor. Or in her purse. Or in her jacket pocket. It took her nearly twenty-five minutes of increasingly anxious searching and feverish speculation (What if she had left them in the lock *outside* her door? Might someone even now be carefully, quietly turning the key, releasing the bolt, preparing to come in?) before she finally located them.

"A place for everything and everything in its place," her mother had drilled into her years ago, and Charlotte had to admit that it made life so much easier when things were kept where they belonged. And like so many of the strictures that narrated her life, Charlotte always followed her mother's rules and admonitions to the letter.

So how *did* her keys end up in the silverware drawer?

"I don't understand," she kept saying, as she put the keys in her pocket and then compulsively patted the bulge to make sure they really *were* there, that they hadn't gone somewhere else. "I always hang them up. I *do*," defending herself against an invisible accuser.

Now her whole Saturday morning schedule was off—that carefully defined routine she had perfected over the years. Leave home at 9:15 sharp, drive to the bank, the post office, and the grocery store before returning home at exactly 11:45.

Then, after allotting another ten minutes to put away the few items she bought—a quart of organic milk, a loaf of whole grain bread, three kosher chicken breasts, and one Spanish onion—she would make a peanut butter sandwich to eat exactly at noon. No jelly, though. Jelly was too unpredictable. It seeped out the sides, dripped off the corners, and in general, made such a mess that Charlotte had decided several years ago that it wasn't worth the trouble.

It wasn't that she didn't *like* jelly. A long time ago, it had been one of her secret pleasures. She loved the way the syrupy liquid would gently envelop her tongue with sweetness and slip into the space between her teeth and the inside of her cheek. Sometimes, hours later, she would slide the tip of her tongue into the corners of her mouth, seeking that last bit of fruity flavor.

But that was when she used to buy it, eat it, enjoy it.

She wasn't sure when she had stopped or why. When she tried to remember, all that came to mind was her mother's voice.

"Sugar is bad for you. It will rot your teeth and upset your stomach and make all kinds of nasty bacteria in your intestines."

Now, every time Charlotte passed the jam and jelly aisle, her mother's words filled her mind the way the fruit used to fill her mouth. But instead of sweetness, there was only a bitter flavor.

Of course, she would tell herself, her mother was only looking out for her, wanting to keep her safe and healthy. That was why, when Charlotte was a child, her mother made very bland but wholesome meals, why she dressed Charlotte in blouses buttoned to the neckline and skirts far too long to ever be considered stylish.

And why she told Charlotte time and again that the best thing she could do to protect herself was to get a job doing something that would limit her contact with other people. Be a file clerk, she would say, or work alone in a bookstore's stockroom, unpacking carton after carton.

"That way, you won't have to deal with them and their unreasonable wants and demands." Their nasty emotions was what she meant but never said. But Charlotte understood her mother's meaning.

And after all, she could hardly blame her since it was one of those nasty emotions that had led to Charlotte's existence.

"The bus was late and the street was deserted and before I knew it—" and there her mother would stop, never completing the story of Charlotte's conception.

But she didn't need to. The blank line for the father's name on Charlotte's birth certificate told her everything she needed to know. And years later, it would be an equally nasty emotion that resulted in her mother's death.

The couple in the late model blue Olds had been arguing, according to the police report, and they never even saw her mother in the crosswalk. They hit her, just like that, and then kept on arguing, while the officers took their statements and the ambulance took her mother.

Granted, her mother shouldn't have been in the roadway. The bystanders said that the flashing red hand clearly indicated that she shouldn't have walked. But still, they should've seen her.

It was so fast, so unexpected. And even though by then Charlotte was a grown woman, her mother's absence created a huge void in her carefully ordered life. She found herself focusing her time and energies on constructing a barricade between herself and the world, doing everything she could to keep herself protected from the unexpected.

But this time, despite all her efforts, the unexpected did occur, and by the time she closed and locked the door behind her (checking three times to make sure it really *was* closed, really *was* locked) and backed her car out of the garage, nearly half an hour had passed.

"Maybe I shouldn't go to the bank today," she said, looking at her watch while she waited for the light to turn green. "That would give me a few extra minutes. But do I have enough money for groceries?"

She started to reach into her purse for her wallet, but just then the light changed and the driver behind her impatiently honked his horn.

Hurriedly, Charlotte stepped on the gas. But although the engine roared, the vehicle itself never moved. She realized too late that she had forgotten to shift it back into drive. Her mother had taught her to always put the car in park when waiting at a stop light, "because your mind could wander and your foot could slip and then the car would go, and then what would happen?"

Something terrible, no doubt, something so bad that Charlotte could not even consider it. And so she never neglected to slide the shifter to "P" when she stopped and then back to "D" before moving her foot from the brake pedal to the accelerator.

Never, until today.

"I'm sorry, I'm sorry," she kept saying (not that the driver could hear her) as she depressed the brake pedal and moved the gearshift, jerking forward before stopping quickly because the light was now red again

She sat there, ashamed, seeing the driver behind her make an obscene gesture, and then tried her best to breathe through the pounding of her heart while waiting for the light to change back to green.

When it did, she moved through the intersection, not daring to look to her left as the man raced past her, not wanting to see his angry face. Her palms, sweaty from fear, kept sliding on the steering wheel, and Charlotte wanted so badly to wipe them on her pants to get that cold wetness off her skin.

But if she did that, if she took her hands, even one at a time, from the wheel, something bad might happen. She might lose control and crash into another car. She might need both hands to turn the wheel to avoid an oncoming vehicle or a bicyclist turning into the road or dog running across the street. She might get a cramp in the hand holding the wheel, and she would be unable to control the direction of the car.

You never know what could happen.

So she gripped the wheel even more firmly and watched the road with rigid attention, eyes darting right–left–right–left, just in case something else might go wrong. And when she pulled into the bank parking lot and finally shut off the engine (triple-checking that the car *was*, in fact, in park), she released the breath she hadn't known she was holding. Then, finally, first one and then the other, she wiped her sweaty palms against her thighs.

She glanced at the car's clock. She was late. Maybe she shouldn't go to the post office. But what if something in her box required immediate attention, like an unexpected bill that needed to be opened and paid right away?

Not that there *should* be a bill because Charlotte was very careful about her expenses. She wrote each one down in a ledger book, carefully noting the amount due, the date to pay it, and finally, the check number and date she discharged the debt.

But still, she really *should* go. And by the time she made up her mind, another ten minutes had passed and her schedule was off by almost three quarters of an hour.

"Do you have your ID?" the teller asked when Charlotte presented the check she wanted to cash—twenty-five dollars—just enough for this week's groceries.

It was the same question every week, but, unlike the other customers, Charlotte had always appreciated the woman's commitment to caution and routine. After all, just because the check had her name on it, just because she looked the same as she had the week before and the week before that, and for all the past weeks and months and years since she had been coming to that branch, still you couldn't be too careful. She might *not* be Charlotte at all, but some other woman who looked just like her—some woman who had somehow gotten into Charlotte's purse and taken her bankbook just to steal twenty-five dollars.

Of course, the only time the bankbook *was* in Charlotte's purse was on Saturdays, because that was the only time she needed it in a public place.

But still, anything might happen.

"Yes, yes, of course," her cheeks flushing because she should have been ready for the question. She should have had her wallet out so she could show the woman her driver's license as soon as she asked for it. Now she would waste precious minutes digging through her purse for her wallet—more minutes than she anticipated because, for some reason, she couldn't find it.

"It's here. It's always here," she said, pushing aside the small flashlight (just in case the lights went out wherever she might be) and pepper spray (in case she was confronted by a mugger) and quarters for the meter (in case there wasn't a free parking space in the post office lot).

"I can't cash it without seeing some form of identification," the teller said.

Charlotte felt a quick burst of anger. The woman *knew* who she was. Charlotte always came to the same window and the same teller every Saturday. Couldn't she make an exception just this once? Charlotte *needed* the money if she was going to buy her groceries And she had get them today. Not Sunday, because she never shopped on Sundays, and not during the week, because the route she followed to and from work took her in a different direction entirely, and she couldn't risk deviating from it in case she got lost and couldn't find her way home.

No, she had to shop today. But how could she without money? And what had happened to her wallet? Fear coursed through her body, drenching her with sweat.

The teller pushed the check back across the counter. "If you find it, I'll be happy to cash your check."

But she wouldn't be happy at all, Charlotte knew. As a matter of fact, she was probably hoping that Charlotte *never* found her wallet and would have to go through the long, laborious, time-consuming process of getting a new driver's license.

Once there, Charlotte would have to explain to the officials that somehow she had lost her original one, at which point they would undoubtedly consider her careless or sloppy. Then she would have to fill out the forms and pay the fee—an unexpected expense that would completely disarrange her budget.

Then the part Charlotte hated most: the vision test. She disliked putting her face in the same chin rest that everyone else used, but was too intimidated by the woman on the other side of the machine to clean the plastic with an antibacterial wipe. The clerk might be offended by the implication that her equipment was dirty. She might even deliberately skew the test results so Charlotte would fail and not get her license.

Then what would Charlotte do? How would she get to the store, the bank, and the post office? And what about *work*? She would be at the mercy of a bus service that was unreliable at best. She would be late punching in and probably lose her job. She wouldn't be able to pay her rent. She'd lose her home and end up on the street!

"Ma'am, if you could step aside so I can wait on someone else."

Charlotte realized she hadn't moved, that the uncashed check was still there for her to retrieve it.

She grabbed the useless slip of paper, knocking over one of several little tchotchkes that were on the counter—a little beaver holding a sign saying, "Thank you for banking on us!"—and turned, clumsily bumping into the man behind her.

"I'm sorry, I'm sorry," she repeated as she left. Once in her car, she dumped out the contents of her handbag, hoping that she had simply overlooked the wallet in the bank.

But it was gone. She had no money, no identification, nothing.

"What should I do?" she asked as though there was someone else in the car who could give her instructions. But there wasn't.

At least, she didn't *think* there was. She had locked the car door. Or had she? She didn't remember unlocking it when she returned. What if she had left it open? What if, even now, someone was hiding in the back seat, waiting for her to leave the lot and go home and pull into her garage? And then, once the overhead door was down, he would come out from behind her and put a knife to her throat or a gun to her head and tell her what he wanted.

Charlotte started to shake. It was possible, even probable, that she had forgotten to lock the door. After all, look how many mistakes she had already made today! It would be just one more in a long line, one final mistake that would completely destroy her ordered world and her with it.

She *could* look. She *could* open the door, and then quickly turn to see if someone were there and if he was, she could leap out of the car and run into the bank. But what if he was gone by the time the bank personnel came out? They would shake their heads and think she was crazy—that crazy woman who first lost her wallet and then claimed to see a stranger in her car.

Or she could slowly get out of the car and, without letting *him* know that she *knew* he was there, start walking—somewhere, anywhere—just walk away and leave her car behind.

But what if he *wasn't* there? What if it was all in her head? How could she return to her car? She'd have to walk back to it—but what if she got lost?

It was now close to 11. She had only forty-five minutes left—not that she could do anything except go to the post office. That's what she'd do: go to the post office and once she was there, she would go inside and stay until it closed at noon.

He'd grow tired of waiting for her and just leave. Maybe she should even leave the keys in the ignition to make it easier for him. Maybe if he took the car, he wouldn't care about Charlotte.

She started the car and slowly backed out of the parking space and headed to the exit.

Was that a rustle from the back? Did she feel a bump against her seat?

Charlotte gripped the steering wheel tightly, her knuckles white against her thin skin. The post office was just a few blocks away; she'd be safe there.

But when she came to the intersection, Charlotte saw that the road on her right was blocked. Orange barricades kept her from turning down the street that led to her destination. One of the road workers waved his hand, directing her to go the other way, but she was afraid to move.

What if the road he was sending her to was blocked as well? What if she got lost and turned the wrong way? What if she couldn't find her way to the post office?

Charlotte looked at her gas gauge, taking no comfort in the fact that it was well past half-full. At this rate, she might be driving all day, using up precious fuel while the man in the seat behind her waited for her to run out of gas and out of places of safety.

And then he would kill her anyway.

"It's all my fault," she said aloud, not caring now if he heard her. She turned then, not the way the worker had pointed but just blindly. It didn't matter which way she went. For all the care she had taken, for all her attention to routine, all her caution, she *still* found herself in danger. And it *was* all her fault. If she hadn't misplaced her keys, if she hadn't left her wallet somewhere, if she hadn't had to sit through another light—if she had only been more cautious, more aware, more alert, *none* of this would have happened.

How many times have I told you to be careful! Her mother's voice echoed in her head.

And Charlotte answered aloud, "I know, I'm sorry, I won't do it again," thinking at the same time that it *wouldn't* happen again because she wouldn't have another chance.

No, she thought, as she drove down one unfamiliar street after another, this was it. This was the end. This was what came of *not* being careful, of *not* paying attention. Bad things happened. And then it was too late.

She made one more turn, this one onto the bypass that circled the city. She had never been on it before but what did it matter? And as she accelerated up the entrance ramp, she wondered how many other places she had never been. Might her life have been different had she been less cautious and more adventurous? Or would the end have only come sooner?

"It doesn't matter," pushing her foot down harder on the gas pedal. And it didn't. Not really.

"No point in looking back," her mother had always said. "You wouldn't like what you see and you can't change it anyway."

No point in looking back, but Charlotte couldn't resist taking a quick glance behind her at the back seat.

It was empty of anything save her fears. Charlotte opened her mouth to sigh in relief...

#

"She never even looked," the driver told the officer. "I saw her coming and slowed down, but I couldn't move over—not *that* fast and besides, there was a tractor-trailer next to me! Where could I go? Why can't people be more *careful?* And she was speeding and not even looking where she was going!

"I saw her face, you know," and he started to shake, seeing again in his mind those eyes, that mouth wide open. "She should have been paying attention, not looking *behind* her! Not on a freeway! After all, anything can happen!"

Out of Sight, Out of Mind

Let me just say at the outset that, in the words of the immortal Bard, this is all much ado about nothing. I pay my taxes—well, I used to pay them when I had anything to pay taxes on—anyway, the taxes I once paid supported public institutions. Like the library. Which means, I maintain, that the aforementioned library—and its roof, in particular—is as much mine as anyone's.

So if I choose to spend one summer night on the asphalt shingles nailed to the library roof, it's entirely my own right and affair.

Besides, I had such a perfect view of the fire from there.

I have always searched for places where I can enjoy some privacy. I believe a person needs time to be alone, to appreciate life and nature and all the wondrous happenings in the world. One night, for instance, I even drove twenty-five miles out to the country, just to revel in the silence and solitude.

(This was before they took my car away, of course—a punishment I found inconvenient, not to mention most unfair. After all, how was I supposed to know the man wouldn't stop for me? The road was built for cars, not pedestrians—crosswalk lines notwithstanding. And he probably wasn't even blind.)

As I was saying, I drove out to the country. It was dark, just a few stars pricking through the black velvet sky. So silent you could hear a pin drop—provided you didn't lose it in the long grass where it wouldn't make a sound that could be heard no matter how quiet it was.

The meadow was lined along one side with tall oak trees—very big, with lots of scratchy bark. Oak trees are so strong, so immovable—just the ticket when the earth suddenly began to rotate a bit faster than normal. I wrapped my arms around the rough trunk and waited to see what would happen next.

Something always happens, it seems.

The rotation built up speed like an out of control merry-go-round. I held on tightly so I wouldn't spin off into the darkness—a helpless victim of centrifugal force. It was frightening but quite exhilarating as well.

I stayed like that for hours, my body pressed against the coarse skin of my rescuer, while the earth spun away in the darkness. And the mad twisting didn't slow until dawn broke over the hillside and cars began appearing on the roadway.

Was the world just tired of turning? Or was it all those bodies that slowed it down, exerting some kind of magnetic force against the wild revolution?

Personally, I think it was the people. It has been my own experience that strange things quit happening when other people are around. Sometimes, it can be very disappointing.

But I digress. As I stated before, the library roof is mine. It's my last stop each evening, after I have let myself through the trapdoor on the grocery store roof to do my nightly shopping.

"Man does not live by bread alone," you know. Milk and eggs and butter are nice to have, too. And since my little home in the woods (actually a large packing crate "borrowed" from a warehouse, but "a rose by any other name...") has neither electricity nor heat, I have to shop every day. If I don't want to starve, that is.

Some would call this stealing. But I'm not one to get caught up in semantics, especially when I'm in the mood for a nice ham and cheese on rye topped with a large deli pickle.

The store is quiet at night. I like that. I can hear the voices so much better when it's quiet. They're clearer, more distinct.

I used to be afraid when I would hear them. After all, no one else could. I thought it meant I was, you know, crazy.

(You see, I can use that word: "crazy." "Sticks and stones may break my bones but words will never hurt me." Although I do remember giving my second-grade teacher a concussion when I hit her with a large edition of Webster's Dictionary. Does that count?)

But then I thought about it—hearing the voices, I mean. After all, you don't get scared when you turn on the radio and disembodied voices come out of the little speakers, do you? Of course not! Then why should I worry because I have mastered the ability to hear voices without benefit of speakers or wires?

Actually, I think it's pretty clever. But I doubt anyone would agree, so I'm keeping this talent to myself. "Discretion *is* the better part of valor."

About the fire—now there they have it all wrong. I certainly didn't set it. Why would I?

It's true that I do harbor some resentment because I wasn't allowed in the store anymore. Accused of causing a disturbance, I was. How ridiculous!

I was just trying to do my shopping, and I intended to pay for everything I took, even the bag of frozen peas slowly defrosting in the pocket of my pants. And I can't help it if, every time I needed to ask the voices for advice, I had to find a deserted aisle so I could hear the answer.

But I certainly *wasn't* talking to myself. *That* would be silly.

I could have argued the point with the store manager but "he who turns and runs away lives to fight another day." Not that it makes any sense, when you think about it. After all, what's the point of escaping if you only have to go through it again at a later date?

But I absolutely, categorically did *not* set the fire. (That's sixteen syllables' worth of denial, in case anyone is counting.)

One does not bite the hand that feeds one. And the store indubitably fed me—and all winter long, kept me warm as well. There is a space behind the water heater on the second floor just large enough for me. I don't take up much room, you know. As a matter of fact, I think I'm getting smaller each day like the character in *The Incredible Shrinking Man*. Not that I've been exposed to large amounts of radiation or dangerous chemicals. At least, not that I know of. On the other hand, do we *really* know what's out there?

I tried explaining all this to the police, who of course refused to believe me. And to be perfectly fair, it *may* have looked a tiny bit suspicious. I did have a rather large supply of matches on me. And my hands did smell a bit like lighter fluid.

Now had I been wearing a three-piece business suit and carrying a briefcase, no one would have accused me of anything. "Clothes make the man," they say. But just because my clothes are ragged and my face is dirty, everyone is willing to entertain the notion that I could be a firebug, an arsonist, a pyromaniac who stayed to watch the building burn.

But my reason for remaining was perfectly understandable. I found the whole scene quite exciting and more than a little entertaining, especially when it became apparent that the fire was getting the best of the firefighters.

No matter which side the fire truck rolled to, it was a safe bet the flames would burn more fiercely on the other. And how the firefighters ran for cover when the gas line ruptured! Certainly better than anything offered on television, and definitely worth the applause I accorded it.

But I was not laughing insanely on the library roof, nor did I shout "*Encore!*" "*Encore!*" when the flames died down. Those damned reporters are notorious for exaggerating the truth.

So now they are keeping me here "under observation," while they search out the cause of the blaze. And since they won't release me, I've decided to not tell them anything—not my name nor where I live—no small piece of information that they could twist to their own advantage.

I refuse to make it easy for them. Let them earn their pay.

But I really would like to get out of here. There's so much noise that I can't hear my voices anymore.

People are laughing, screaming, crying. There's nowhere to go to have any silence.

And I badly need their advice—my voices, I mean. They help me so much. You know, if it wasn't for them, I wouldn't have known how to make a small bonfire from rags and kerosene to simultaneously celebrate Midsummer's Eve and cook foot-long hot dogs.

It was an excellent idea. And if I hadn't gotten sidetracked in the produce department (so many ears of corn to choose from just to find the perfect one to roast!), I'm sure I would have made it back before the flames had gotten too far out of hand.

But I didn't. Obviously. So now I'm operating on the "least said, soonest mended" principle. I hope it works. Once I'm out of here, I'm sure I'll be able to hear my voices again. My life will get back to normal and I can forget all about the padded walls and straitjackets and long, sharp needles.

I have always been very good at forgetting unpleasant things. Once I get away from them, they are buried and forgotten.

After all, you know what they say: "Out of sight, out of mind."

Misconnections

They blamed the airplane crash on "equipment failure." Some little cog or pin or cylinder had failed to move when it was supposed to, and so the connection was not made in time.

Mechanical misconnection. Crash. Burn.

I had purposely avoided watching any part of the televised reports because I was afraid I would dream about it. But the information couldn't be avoided. The news was everywhere: on the radio, in the paper, and part of everyone's conversation. And so the dreams came.

I was watching rescue workers at the scene of the plane crash. One woman, dressed in a starched white nurse's uniform, was bringing from the wreckage small stained bundles that turned out to be dead infants.

I remember the sticky film of blood and bodily fluids when she unwrapped them, and I wondered why there were so many dead babies on the plane.

When I arose the next morning, I saw my bedsheet was stained with pink. My period had come—unexpectedly, but not undesired. My husband and I didn't want any more children; we had agreed on that. That was why the IUD scraped me clean with efficient regularity.

No babies to be born, no fertilized eggs connecting to a nutrient-filled lining.

Disconnection. Removal.

So why did I have the dream?

I have never had much luck understanding the hidden messages behind my nocturnal imaginings. Sometimes, I could brush them off in the light of day like so many cobwebs—vague and insubstantial. Others were not so easy to dismiss. They lingered like a damp fog chilling my bones. Some, like the dreams of phone calls from some unnamed person, return again and again to haunt me.

I can remember one of the dreams: "What now, Anna?" the voice reaching to my ears through the wires.

As I held the receiver, a hand snaked out of the mouthpiece to fasten around my wrist. The fingers were cold and unyielding.

"What now, Anna?" insistently, and then the line went dead.

When I awoke, I was lying rigid, my fingers clenched together, my body drenched with sweat. For a moment, I thought to awaken my husband. But he wouldn't understand.

I have asked my husband if he dreams, but he says he does not. I have watched him, on those nights when I can't sleep, and seen his face change and his eyelids twitch, and wonder where his mind is roaming. But he says he does not dream.

My children dream though. I know this because they have inherited my ability to walk and talk in their sleep, carrying on conversations and moving from one room to the next with the stubborn irrationality of the somnambulist.

As I'd guide them back to bed, tuck them in and close the door, I wondered what kind of dream world held them captive, what possibilities existed for them in their night-time fantasies.

When I was young, my dream-life was so active that my parents fastened extra chains on the doors to keep me in the house. I was always trying to leave— go somewhere, see someone. The world held so many possibilities that daylight hours were not sufficient.

Now I dream of sorrow, loss, pain. I have killed off and buried every member of my family in my dreams: been present at their funerals or received the news second-hand through the phone wires. My father alone has died three times that I can remember.

After the last dream, I called my parents, but heard only their greeting on the answering machine: "We aren't in right now. Leave your name and number, and we'll call you back."

I wanted to ask, "Are you alive or dead?" But my parents are in their seventies, and I didn't wish to alarm them.

So I waited until they returned from what was yet another road trip. By now, they have crisscrossed Florida so many times that tracing their journey on a map would result in an overlapping series of pencil lines, like a child's game of cat's cradle.

And, after so many trips, their roles are carefully delineated. My mother packs, unpacks, re-packs. My father carries suitcases out to the car, checks his watch, and sighs loudly enough for my mother to hear. Other people have clocks to keep track of the time. My mother knows the time by the length of my father's sighs.

In the car, my father drives and my mother talks. One activity is totally unrelated to the other, and they are both satisfied merely with the other's physical presence. I know from experience that there will occasionally be cross words, arguments even, revolving around the adjustment of the airflow from the vents, the speed of the car, the amount of stops between origin and destination.

But these are merely misfirings of an otherwise well-tuned engine. After all the years together, there are enough working connections to keep the motor running.

Once they were home, I called again: "How was your trip? Were the roads busy? Are my nephews taller?" (Are you still alive, or have you died and no one has told me yet?)

"The trip was fine," my mother answered. "Of course, your father drove too fast—you did, dear, even the patrolman said so! But the scenery was beautiful. You should drive down someday with the children."

But we don't make car trips—not after the first and last vacation we took. The children fought all the way—an endless eight-hour bickering. Their motors were racing, and there was no way to slow them down.

All during that endless drive, my husband gripped the steering wheel so tightly his knuckles turned white, his lips set shut.

The return journey was more peaceful. The children, tired after eight days of beachcombing and swimming, occupied themselves with souvenirs. In the quiet, I could hear the radio station playing a song my husband and I had once danced to.

He glanced over at me and then reached out to hold my hand—an unaccustomed gesture of affection. But my fingers were greasy from the fries I had been eating, and, after a moment, he released me.

Equipment failure.

That night I dreamed again of the airplane crash. This time, though, there was a girl, no more than three or four, wearing only white training pants, her short golden curls tangled around her face.

She walked, with the precision the young sometimes show in unfamiliar territory, until she came to an empty stretcher waiting on the stony ground. For a long time she stood in front of it, one finger probing inside her mouth, and a look of intense concentration on her face.

She didn't have a mark on her: no scratches, no scrapes, no burns. But I knew she had been on the plane and had somehow crawled unharmed from the wreckage.

Finally, her fingers found what they were searching for, and she drew out of her mouth one very small baby tooth, loosened perhaps in the crash. Carefully, she laid it on the stretcher, and then stood there gazing at it, waiting, I suppose, for the Tooth Fairy to bring her some coins.

Only the young can hope like that—without reason, without proof. If I once held that much hope in my heart, it has faded away. Now I only believe in what I can see and taste and feel. That is what's real— not hope, not dreams.

And yet, as I stirred my coffee in the early morning hours, I wondered if she was waiting there still.

Dreams—even the truly dead cannot escape my dreams. I bring them back to life, where we talk and embrace, exchange love and words, re-connect after years apart, only to say goodbye again.

When I awake, they are still dead. That is the trade-off I am granted: the alive remain living, despite my dream-murders, but the dead must stay dead.

Lately, I had been waking with sleep-induced headaches and heavy eyes. My doctor prescribed small blue pills "to relax me." They took away the dreams, leaving my mind empty and washed clean, like the land after some terrible flood.

The feeling would remain into the daylight hours, and I found I was losing track of what day it was— what week, what month. Sometimes, last year and yesterday seemed interchangeable, as indistinct as faraway trees in a gray fog.

I didn't feel tired anymore. I didn't feel anything anymore.

So I stopped taking the pills, preferring the exhaustion of my dreams to the terrible emptiness.

During the day, I do what other women do. I shop for groceries, wash clothes, and make beds. I dust the furniture, run the vacuum, and plan the evening meal. I watch the afternoon soaps, the six o'clock news, and the evening sitcoms. I go to bed with my husband of fifteen years, lying down on crisp cotton sheets and feather pillows.

Sometimes, my husband falls asleep right away, snoring into the pillow, while I lie awake, watching him. Sometimes, we make love, a carefully orchestrated dance of bodies and hands—connecting physically but not emotionally. Not anymore.

When we are done, he pats my shoulder the way one would pat a mare after a day's exercise, and then pulls the sheet around himself and turns away.

I want to cry, but I don't. I wouldn't be able to explain the tears, even if he would ask. He doesn't mean to hurt me. But there you have it. I am hurt anyway.

Movement out of sync. Engine out of tune. Damage.

And on the following mornings, he would be especially kind to me. He is a kind man, but, on those mornings, there is an extra sense of gentleness about him—which is why I never refuse to make love to him. Gentleness, even when it is a substitute for love, is not a thing one can refuse—not in this world, where mindless cruelty is so common, where random failures can destroy unsuspecting lives.

I know I am fortunate. I have healthy children and a responsible husband. If I want more, I keep it to myself, lest what I already have be taken as a punishment for my greed.

Tonight I had another dream: the phone rang and when I answered, I heard a single question—"What do you want?" Then nothing more, and when I awoke, the question was still echoing in my mind.

What do I want?

I looked around me—at fifteen years of furniture and wall coverings, at fifteen years of marriage and family life, at fifteen years of connections.

"I don't know," and I turned, hugging my husband's body for warmth.

Skating on Thin Ice

"For the twelfth straight day, the high will only reach the single digits, setting a new record—"

I turn off the radio before I could hear the rest of the forecast. When I was a child, weather like this meant the pond behind my parents' house would be frozen—glass-smooth and hard as tempered steel. We would gather on the shore, where some kind neighbor had lit a bonfire, and alternately toast our faces and our backsides while strapping on the high-topped, sharp-bladed skates.

The unsafe portions of the ice were clearly marked. Ominous red flags warning "Weak Ice" were posted on the thinner surface, and stiff brown ropes were strung from pole to pole, confining the young to the safer areas.

As a child, I obeyed the warning. But in the invulnerable teenage years, I joined friends in daring each other to leap the cord and try our luck on the melting surface.

Most of the time, our luck held. Skate lines crisscrossed each other in ever-deepening slices, and sometimes the rifle-sharp crack from below the surface would scare us back behind the rope. But never for very long. First one, then another would tip-toe on skate point, and, seeing no widening breach, no ominous fluid darkness, venture back onto the thin ice.

But luck cannot be tempted indefinitely without demanding payment. The year I turned fifteen, eight older boys played crack-the-whip on the unsafe section, sending one of their own sailing out alone under the moonlight. A widening black line followed him, but there wasn't enough time for him to come back to safety. And, in the end, he was simply swallowed up like a long-awaited meal.

"*Paul! Paul!*"

The shouts echoed across the darkening night until someone had the presence of mind to call a parent, the police, the ambulance.

By then, it was too late.

There was no more skating on the pond after that, and the following summer, the neighbors banded together to hire an excavating company to fill it in—the largest single gravesite I have ever seen.

I have since learned that thin ice is not only a condition of winter nor confined to stretches of frozen water. There is thin ice everywhere—between lovers and friends, between reality and obsession, between hope and despair.

And sometimes, the only warning you receive is the sharp crack just before the ice breaks and you fall through—to nowhere.

When I was five years old, we moved from the sunshine and sand of southern Florida to this cold state of Ohio. It was January, and bare tree limbs cast stark shadows against the whitened landscape. Snow was an unfriendly stranger—chilling my suntanned skin, reddening my face—and the dazzling reflection of the sun off its white surface was painfully bright.

My father took me ice-skating on the park's frozen pond. Not because he wished to spend time with me, but to escape the house where my mother was.

My mother was "sleeping." My mother always "slept" in the afternoon. Among the many bags and boxes we brought in our battered Ford wagon was the hidden truth of my mother's sickness.

At sixteen, I would say my mother was a drunk. Twenty years later, I could say she was an alcoholic. But the right words, like my compassion and understanding, are two decades too late.

Hurriedly, my father strapped the borrowed skates onto my feet. But they were too big, and like an ungainly bird, I flapped my wool-covered wings to keep my balance.

"Come on," and impatiently, he grabbed at my hand, towing me out to the center where other families swirled and dipped in an unfamiliar dance. I held onto him tightly, and, following his terse instructions, slid my feet tentatively across the cold glassy surface.

And for a moment, I was dancing, too.

Then, my skate caught in a crack and I stumbled. My father's fingers, never holding very tightly, released their grip as I fell to my knees. For a moment, I thought the crack I heard was the sound of the ice breaking, and that I would soon fall through the widening slice to vanish forever into the frozen depths.

But it was only my ankle that was broken. I stayed, a frozen bird trapped in the ice, until my father finally turned and saw that I had fallen. For a moment, he paused, as though deciding whether or not to come back. The late afternoon sunshine illuminated him, and I understood then that, each day, he must make the decision to return.

It was not only my ankle that hurt. It was not only the fragile bone that had been broken.

#

"He's gone and left us, the dirty bastard!"

My mother stood there on the porch in her threadbare housecoat, the November wind whipping it against her blue-veined legs.

I quickly turned around, hoping no one from school was near enough to see her or hear her voice, slurred and thickened with alcohol and rage.

I knew, without having to ask, what had happened. I had seen my father packing late the night before. But he didn't see me. His mind was a hundred miles away—probably in some other house, with some other woman.

"Mom, go back inside."

But she ignored me, hugging her arms around herself as if to hold in what little warmth her scrawny body could generate.

My mother was painfully thin, almost a wraith. Sometimes I wondered how she had the strength to go on living. Sometimes I wished she didn't.

I opened the door, throwing my schoolbooks onto the kitchen table, and then came back to lead her into the house.

"The dirty bastard," she repeated, and tears ran down her face. I set her gently on a chair, brought her a pill and some vodka, wiped her tears away.

The next morning, I called my school to tell them in a grown-up voice that "little Sarah is sick with the flu and will have to stay home the rest of the week"— the first, but not the last time I played that role.

Sometimes, I thought they knew it was me, pretending to be my mother. But if they investigated the situation, they might have had to do something, accept some responsibility, take some action. And they were already too busy with other problems.

So, they took me at my word, and I bought time to stay with my mother until she was well enough for me to leave during the day.

"Why did he leave me?" and the tears started again, the low keening a mourning chant for a dead marriage.

I turned on the overhead light, seeing in its ruthless glare the dirty dishes in the sink, the broken glass scattered across the floor.

"He'll be back," I said automatically and began to sweep up the glittering shards. Then, while she continued to sob, I heated some canned soup and toasted stale bread.

In spite of the grief permeating the kitchen, I was hungry.

#

Drinking, like breathing or sleeping, came naturally to my mother.

After a few glasses—vodka, mostly but occasionally gin—my mother would fall asleep, her snores echoing through the house. She would sleep anywhere and everywhere: at the kitchen table, on the faded couch in the cold living room, once even in the bathtub, while the water rose higher and higher around her weak, ugly body.

I tried moving her from the tub, but her wet flesh was too slippery. And she wouldn't answer me, no matter how much I raised my voice.

"Mom! Mom, come on. You have to *move*. Mom!" my voice growing sharper as the frustration built. "Wake up! You can't stay in here."

I slapped her face—not once but several times—but her head lolled like a rag doll's. Finally, I left her there, in the cooling water, and went back to my homework.

By morning, the bathtub was empty, and I was able to shower before leaving for school.

#

When I was sixteen, I tasted liquor for the first time. It wasn't my first flirtation with a vice—I had been smoking since I was twelve. There was never a need to hide it from anyone. My mother would not have noticed it, and my father was too far away to care what I did. But lately, cigarettes failed to provide me with what I needed.

Spending a night at a friend's house, I went with her into the darkened dining room, crowded with heavy mahogany furniture.

"What would you like?" and, one by one, she set the bottles on the lace tablecloth.

I tried whiskey first, but it burned my tongue and brought tears to my eyes. My mother preferred vodka, but I found it too numbing, flavorless yet powerful. Finally, I reached for the wine.

I wrestled with the cork, then, once it was opened, I tipped the bottle to my lips, pushing aside the bits of cork with my tongue and letting the liquid slip into my mouth.

As I swallowed, I gazed critically at the bottle. The label was pretty—a pastoral scene with trees and horses. It was supposed to reassure the drinker that the liquid was healthy, fermented as it was from fruits ripening in the sunshine. The wine tasted more of alcohol than fruit, but I didn't mind. After all, it wasn't flavor that I was seeking.

My friend turned on the crystal chandelier, and I saw myself reflected in the lace-curtained window— eyes like dark holes in the pale circle that was my face. Watching myself, I tipped the bottle to my lips again.

#

There were not many choices open to a woman thirty years ago. High school was followed by either clerical work or college, depending on the female's intelligence, motivation, and finances. But the ultimate goal was the same for nearly all: to be married to a reasonably handsome, steadily employed husband and bear him two-point-five children.

That was the acceptable path, the mark of success. But, for some of us, the path wasn't so straight and clear. Sometimes, it deviated, and the sequence of events became scrambled and out of sync.

"Are you sure?" he asked.

My hands were slippery on the black receiver. These were not the words I wanted to hear. This was not the tone of voice I had hoped for.

"Of course I am." My voice was more confident than I felt. It was, after all, not an unheard of situation. It had happened before—to other girls, other couples. The colleges were full of new-marrieds with babies on the way.

"The doctor says I should be just fine."

"You're young. You're healthy," were his exact words. He had shoved a prescription for vitamins into my cold hands. "I'll see you in one month. Any questions? No? Good."

No, I had no questions, not even if I should stop drinking the Bloody Marys that had become a part of my daily diet. If I had asked him, he might have dismissed its importance. Alcoholism was not something discussed in polite society. Besides, his lunches were also liquid—vodka Martinis, I'd heard.

The silence from the other end was deafening. I twisted the cord around my wrist, waiting.

Then, "What are you going to do?" and I heard the pronoun the way one hears the guillotine right before it slices away life.

"I thought..." and my voice died away. I thought—what? That he would marry me? That my life would have a form, a shape, some semblance of normalcy? That I could have my drinks in the privacy of my own living room, rather than sneaking the bottles into a crowded dorm?

That I would never be alone again?

"I can give you some money to, you know..." and I understood then that it was my problem to deal with—mine and mine alone.

I uncoiled the cord and gently hung the phone back onto the metal holder. There were red marks on my wrist where the cord had cut into my skin. Later that night, I would recreate those lines with the blade of my scissors.

They told me I was fortunate. And, contrite and frightened, he came to see me. We were married three weeks later, before I began to fill out the front of my dress.

But it ended, as it began, with a sharp unexpected pain and trails of blood. An ambulance ride, sirens screaming, lights flashing. The examining room was blindingly bright, and I closed my eyes against the glare of the round lamp, wishing I could close my body against the doctor's ice-cold instruments.

We had no need to buy baby furniture after all. Later, in our small apartment's darkened living room, I swallowed medicine and tranquilizers, washing them down with spiked tomato juice. After two drinks, I didn't notice whether or not he came home. After a few more, I didn't even care.

#

In what ultimately became a vain attempt to escape from our past, my husband and I had moved far from the town where we had gone to college, farther still from my mother, who clung to her bitter memories in the house by the pond.

Sometimes, while watching other mothers wheel baby carriages in the park, I could almost convince myself that the childhood I recalled had never existed—that somewhere in my past was another mother: normal, stable, sober.

But then a late night or early morning phone call would destroy the fantasy I had created. My mother's voice, cracked and harsh, would pull me back into the alcohol-blurred past.

"You never come to see me," she would begin, and I would reach for my glass and take a long drink, knowing I would need it. "You're like your father— you used me and left me all alone. What kind of daughter are you?" and her voice would rise and fall, a tide of words eating away at the bulwarks I had erected.

Sometimes the silence would stretch out for long minutes, and I imagined her pouring yet another drink, lighting yet another cigarette. I wondered if she would catch fire someday, all that alcohol inside her feeding the flames until she blazed into nothingness.

If I were a better daughter, I would try to help her. If I were a stronger person, I would put immeasurable miles between us—refuse to accept her calls, her grief, my guilt. But I was neither. I was only my mother's daughter, listening to her litany of pain and accusations, wondering if I had enough alcohol to last through the afternoon.

Even when the call was over, when the phone rested back in its cradle, I could see her face, hear her voice, smell the alcohol on her breath. It would take several more drinks before I would stop seeing, hearing, smelling my mother.

#

Marriage has been described as an institution as though it were a building that housed sick people or inmates. For me, it had been a place in which to exist, a wall to hide behind.

But over the years, my marriage, never very strong, had developed cracks in the foundation. Small breaks: the phone numbers scribbled on slips of paper, unexplained because I was afraid to question. Larger breaks: the workdays stretching later into the night, the business trips growing more frequent. On bad days, I believed I could feel our marriage quivering, waiting for the one last tremor that would shake it to pieces.

Those were the days when I slept late and went to bed early. Alcohol was my solution, my salvation.

"I can't put up with this anymore!" My husband's voice shook the house, reverberating in my ears until I thought I would be deafened. "You do nothing but drink—day in and day out!"

I didn't know what to answer, so I sipped my drink instead. But he slapped the glass from my hand, and then, harder, slapped my face.

"Listen to me!"

I turned my head up toward where I imagined his face to be. It's hard to see clearly after three in the afternoon. Or maybe it was just hard to see after three.

"Look at you," and he dragged me to the bathroom mirror. The overhead light hurt my eyes, but he made me look. But instead of my own reflection, it was my mother's I saw.

"I need a drink."

Defeated, he let me go.

"I want out—out of this life, out of this marriage. It's over between us. You can have the house. I'm leaving."

I understood what he was saying. It sounded familiar, like I had heard it all before, long ago. I poured half a glass of vodka and took a long swallow. Then I turned to him.

"Dirty bastard" and I threw the glass across the room, watching it shatter against the wall.

#

"I need to speak with Sarah Armstrong."

I turned on the bedside lamp, the glare from the bulb burning my eyes. I blinked them a few times,

119

trying to ease the dryness, before shifting the receiver closer to my mouth.

"Yes, what do you want?" My voice was rough, and I cleared my throat before continuing. "This is Sarah Armstrong. What is it?"

"We have a patient here—Anna Wilson."

"My mother," I said quickly. It had been several years since I had been to see her. The nursing supervisor had said she didn't recognize anyone anymore, that I didn't have to make the three-hour trip if I didn't want to.

I had grasped at the escape that she offered like a drowning man clutches at a rope. I didn't want to see my mother. I didn't want to watch her shaking hands or look at her face crisscrossed with spider veins. I didn't want to see myself.

"Mrs. Armstrong, I am sorry to tell you that your mother passed away last night."

I wanted to tell her that my mother had died years ago, that all they had been feeding and washing and medicating was an empty body. But I had enough control over my tongue to stay silent.

It was a good thing that she called at that time. Sometimes, by late afternoon, when I've had a few more drinks, I say things I shouldn't. At least, that was what my husband used to tell me.

"…make the arrangements," and I understood that she had been talking to me, that I had missed something of importance.

"I'm sorry," and the words hung in the air. "I'm sorry," I repeated. "Could I call you back? I need... I need..."

My voice trailed off uncertainly, and she mistook my silence for grief.

"Of course, and please accept our deepest sympathy," she said warmly. "We'll wait to hear from you."

I hung up the phone and wondered if my mother had remembered the little girl with straight brown hair who would bring her coffee laced with vodka.

#

"Why don't you watch where you're going?"

The shout brought me back to the present, to the danger of cars passing far too closely. I stepped back onto the curb, wondering why I had ever left the safety of its shallow elevation.

It was nearly six o'clock, and the glare of the setting sun brought tears to my eyes.

"I'm sorry," I said, but the driver had already moved on. I walked more carefully, gauging my steps, holding fast to my handbag. All I wanted was to make it to the corner and around to the side street. There was a place where I could stay for a few hours. They knew me.

Before long, I was seated on a corner stool in the darkened bar. I drank the vodka straight—no ice, no lime. It took three drinks before my hands stopped shaking, one more before I could face the mirrored wall behind the bottles.

I had not expected to feel so bereft, so alone. For years, I had struggled against her needs, hoping her death would give me release. But nothing had changed.

My face swam above the row of bottles—white skin, dark eyes. The image shifted and altered, and I

121

thought I could see the outlines of my skull behind the flesh. And, behind that, my mother's face.

The mirror was dark and cloudy—like ice on a storm-crossed winter afternoon. Even in the crowded bar, where bodies pressed tightly against one another, I felt chilled. I took another sip, and the image shifted again. I could almost see the break in the glassy surface. I could almost hear the sharp crack as the ice began to give way.

"Lady, you want another?" and I realized that my glass was almost empty. "Hey, lady, I'm asking you—do you want another drink?"

"No," and I stepped unsteadily down from the barstool onto the carpeted floor, onto dry land. "No, I've had enough."

#

They say the cold snap will continue for at least a few more days. Motorists are cautioned that roads are still slippery, and schools close early or open not at all.

But the below-freezing temperatures do not deter the children. Each afternoon, I watch from my apartment as they make their way to the park across the road. Some drag sleds, willing to struggle up the snow-covered hill just for the exhilaration of a twenty-second flight down the powdery whiteness.

Others, carrying skates, head for the small pond. There, signs indicate where the ice is strong enough to support all those daring bodies, all those sharp blades.

If the children are careful—if they obey the rules and warnings—they won't crack the surface to fall into the darkness.

If I am careful, neither will I.

NANCY CHRISTIE

Still Life

This is how it should be—

In the morning, I would go into my kitchen with its golden oak cabinets and white tile counter tops, where I would grind some fine brown coffee beans— a special blend, grown high in the Andes where the air is so sharp it can slice your lungs. When the coffee has finished brewing, I would pour it into a delicate gold-rimmed demitasse, and the steam would rise, rich and fragrant, almost as satisfying as that very first taste.

I would take my cup and one freshly baked, flaky croissant, and walk out onto the deck. From there, I would watch the sun as it fights its way through the pine trees, struggling to reach the sky. The first rays color the darkness orange and red, purple and gold, and as the night is conquered, the sun would emerge victorious.

On the deck, there is one small glass-topped table with wrought iron legs, a wicker rocker with a thick purple-flowered seat cushion, and my easel.

I look at the sky and then at my paint box and colored pencils, waiting on the shelf below the empty canvas. Finally, with slow, deliberate strokes, I begin to sketch my world—the pines, with each needle meticulously placed on each branch and each branch grafted carefully onto the trunk, and the sky: its colors melting and bleeding into each other like a dying harlequin.

While I work, the kittens would come out to investigate the world in which they find themselves. The white one—the baby, I call her—immediately leaps into the rocker and settles down, her tail curling around like a mask to hide her face. Her blue eyes would move back and forth, watching me as I bring the sun and sky onto the canvas.

The black kitten would first twine around my ankles, tickling my skin with his tail, before vaulting onto the wooden railing. He is as much at ease as though it was six feet wide instead of six inches, as though the ground was not twenty feet below.

He would pace along the edge, a jungle predator hunting for food, until, tired of the game, he joins his mate in the chair where they sleep together—black and white, night and day—curled into a furry circle.

There is no radio, no telephone, no sound except the wind and the birds and the stream, far below and hidden by the underbrush. I can hear the water, even high on my deck, rushing and tumbling over rocks worn smooth by its endless caress.

Later, when I grow tired of standing at the easel, I would slip into a pair of old soft jeans, and walk through the woods in search of blackberries for lunch. With moccasins in hand, I ford the stream where minnows tease my toes and waterbugs dance on the sparkling surface.

When I reach the other side, I push through the brambles and wild rose bushes to find the meadow where the blackberries grow. Here, in the open sunlight, they are ripe to bursting, and I am painted purple and red as I pluck them, resisting, from their stems. I gather them in my basket and slip them in my mouth, tasting the morning sun on my tongue.

Later again, much later, I would relax in my rocking chair, drinking champagne from a delicately etched crystal goblet, watching the stars glitter in the darkening sky. The fireflies dance and dart around the edges of the deck, and moths eagerly, willingly dive to their deaths into the white pillar candle burning in a hand-thrown pottery bowl.

I would stretch out my legs before me, scratched and tired from the afternoon walk, and rest my head on the back of the chair. My fingers are tinted with sunrise colors, the paint permanently stained into my skin from endless mornings spent at my easel, and I can no longer remember the true color of my flesh.

#

I think about this dream life on cold rainy mornings while I am waiting for the water to boil. When the steam rises from the kettle's aluminum spout, I make my coffee, stirring bubbling water into the dull black crystals waiting at the bottom of the chipped, stained cup.

I have ten minutes to drink my coffee, another ten minutes allotted for the stairs, and ten more for the walk to the corner bus stop. There I wait, amid blaring horns and choking exhaust fumes, early-morning drunks and street people curled like rags on the steam grate.

This is how it is.

The Storyteller

"When I was a little girl, we lived in a big stone farmhouse on the outskirts of the city. In the barn behind the house, there were three cows, two sheep, and a horse we called Lightning because when he ran, his hooves would draw sparks from the stony path."

The children gathered around Connie when she began telling her stories and for a brief time they'd forget the needles and the pills, the cold examining table, and the way they could never really tell what the doctors were thinking while they poked and prodded.

Connie took them away from the green-walled prison that was their home to a place where children ran freely in knee-high grass, not shuffle like old men down linoleum-floored halls, dragging IV poles along with them like uprooted trees.

"Did your sheep have names?" It was Carla, always Carla, who interrupted the story to get the details clear. Carla wanted answers to all her questions, even the most unanswerable one of all: why?

"One was called Fluffy and the other Muffy," Connie answered obligingly. Those weren't good names, but they'd be easy to remember. She had to keep all the details consistent. The children would notice any changes, any misnamed animals or misplaced buildings, and then the fabric of the story would disintegrate.

"Every morning, my father would go outside and milk the cows that were standing in the fragrant straw.

126

The cows liked being milked. They knew how important it was to give rich cream for butter and warm milk for my oatmeal. And they liked the way my father would stroke their sides after he was through, telling them what good animals they were, and how much they were needed. Because of them, we always had plenty of milk in the house."

When they needed milk in the house (which was most of the time), Connie would pick through the debris on her father's dresser searching for enough money to buy another quart.

Sometimes, there was enough. But, more often than not, the money for milk and other necessities would have been swallowed up with the beer he drank each day after work. Then, she would have to have bread for breakfast, with cold water to wash down the day-old slices.

"Did you have a dog, Grandma Connie?" Jesse asked.

Jesse had a dog once, Connie knew. But a doctor had told his parents that it was the cause of his sickness, and so they had it put to sleep, telling Jesse that they had given it away. But he told Connie he had overheard them talking one night and he knew that was a lie.

And it turned out that it wasn't the dog's fault after all, but the fault of an unnamed sickness hidden deep inside of his body.

"Yes, we had a dog," she answered gently. "But he was an outside dog"—Jesse's had slept at the foot of his bed—"and he would guard the sheep and the cows and horse."

"Do you have any pictures?" Carla asked.

Connie shook her head. "No, we didn't have a camera. But my mother painted pictures of the farm and the animals. They are at my son's house now, or I'd bring them to you."

Connie's mother had left the year the young girl turned eight. "I can't take it anymore!" Connie heard her scream one night after her father had come stumbling home. "You drink all the time and there's never enough money for me and the kid!"

"I'm leaving, Jack! I've had it!"

"Where does your son live?" It was Jason, the new boy. He had been admitted a few days before, but until today, the tests had left him too weak to attend Connie's afternoon story hour in the playroom. He sat there in the small wheelchair, pale-faced and fragile, though his eyes burned with life.

"Down south," Connie answered, wondering if she had answered this question about her mythical son before and in which state she had placed him. "South" was a good choice—a place none of the children had gone, far from this cold state and colder hospital.

Connie would make up descriptions of her son's house and garden, the way the heat shimmered on the pavement in the middle of July and the magnolia blossoms filled the air with their scent. Sometimes, after a particularly detailed description of the brilliant sunlight dancing on the fast-rushing stream at the edge of town, the children's faces would glow, as though a bit of the southern warmth had touched them.

"He has two children: a little girl named Sally and a little boy named Joey. Joey plays baseball in the summer and Sally has a white kitten with four black paws."

The children loved those little details. They needed them to flesh out the pictures of Connie's life. She had become their window to another world, where they too could play in the barn or run races with Sally and Joey.

There were times when Connie would close her eyes and see her imaginary son and grandchildren. She'd hear their voices and feel their kisses upon her cheek.

"I'm sorry, Mrs. Smrenak, but having children just isn't possible, I'm afraid. There seems to be some problem with your—" the doctor had paused there, searching for the right words to delicately describe the problem with Connie's body, "your female parts. I think it might be a good idea to have some tests done to see what the problem is. It might turn out to be nothing very bad at all," he had added with a false heartiness that didn't fool Connie for a minute.

The tests were painful, and the operation that followed was even worse. Her husband had stood at the foot of the bed, holding his hat and not meeting her eyes. This wasn't part of the deal, she knew. People got married to have children, but she hadn't lived up to her end of the bargain.

He never reproached her for her failure, and she never complained about his drinking, even when the doctor warned him it would kill him. And in the end he became like a child—needy, dependent, cantankerous. When he died, she wasn't certain if she felt relief or sorrow. Or maybe both.

It wasn't the life Connie had wanted, but then, few things went the way one wished. She knew this, and looking into the children's eyes, she could see they knew it as well. Knew it and accepted it.

"Grandma Connie, could I see you a moment?"

It was the afternoon supervisor. Connie frowned. She didn't like being interrupted in the middle of her storytelling time, partly because the children grew restless while they waited for her, and partly because it was difficult to remember where she had left off. But she pulled herself out of the rocker and obediently went to the nearby office.

The woman shut the door and then took a seat behind the desk, smiling at Connie in the false way the children would have recognized: *Now, this isn't going to hurt a bit. Just one prick and it will all be over.*

But it always hurt. Sometimes it hurt a lot. Sometimes it wasn't just one little prick but a long piercing pain that went on and on.

Connie sat stiffly in the straight-backed chair and waited.

"You know we appreciate the time you spend with our patients. The children really enjoy the stories about your childhood."

Connie breathed in. This was the alcohol-swab part, when the skin is made ready for the hypodermic needle.

"We recognize that sometimes medicine isn't enough. The children need emotional nourishment, and often the parents are so stressed that they are incapable of giving any more to the children."

Now the needle is filled with medicine, and the plunger is depressed, just a little, until some of the liquid shoots from the silver tip. Connie tightened her jaw. *It's coming now—the part that would hurt.*

"So we've decided to bring in some professional play therapists to work with the children. They have books and games that will not only entertain the patients, but also help them express their feelings in a healing way. It's not that we don't appreciate all you have done in the past few months"—and now the needle is plunged deep into the skin, hurting, hurting—"but we feel that a professional will be better able to handle the children's needs. I'm sure you understand—"

There, it didn't hurt a bit, did it, dear? Now, wipe your eyes and go play.

"When?" Connie interrupted her brusquely, and the woman looked away, slightly embarrassed. Really, it was just too much to expect her to handle this. This wasn't *her* job, after all. She wasn't the one who had accepted this old lady as a volunteer in the first place.

"Tomorrow," she answered, fiddling with the paper knife on her desk. "I don't see any need to tell the children. We'll keep them so busy that they'll hardly notice," not realizing how cruel the words were and how wrong she was.

The children would most certainly notice, Connie knew. Jesse would see Connie's departure as one more thing he loved and lost. Sometimes, when Connie would stop in to see him on her way home to her one-bedroom walk-up, she would find him clutching his stuffed bear and crying for his lost puppy. She had promised him that, when he was better, he could come visit her and her little dachshund Daisy.

Connie didn't have a pet. But it was a safe lie to tell, because Jesse wasn't going to get better. That was another lie, too.

Carla would drive the therapist wild with her questions: "Where did Grandma Connie go?" "Why isn't she coming back?" "Why didn't she say goodbye?"

The therapist would give her a different answer each day, and Carla would grow more and more angry, and then the tantrums would begin again: toys thrown across the room, crayons smashed into a million colored bits, aides scratched and bitten as they tried to wash her and comb her thin hair.

Carla never behaved that way with Connie because Connie always answered her—sometimes with complete truthfulness, sometimes with a falsehood that was better than the truth. But she always tried to satisfy Carla's desire to know the simple things, because the most important question had no answer at all.

"I would like to finish the story hour now," Connie said, and without waiting for an answer, she made her way back to the children.

"What did she want?" Carla asked, and Connie patted her on the head.

"Well, I have a little bit of news for you children," she began slowly. She saw the supervisor in the doorway, ready to intervene. "There was a call from my son—you remember, he lives down south—"

"With little Joey and Sally and Sally's kitten," Jesse said, and Connie smiled.

"That's right, with Joey and Sally and Sally's kitten. Remember how I told you that Joey played baseball?"

The children nodded.

"Well, Joey was running to catch the ball and he tripped right over his own feet and fell smack on the ground. And he hurt his arm—"

"Did he break it? Will they have to cut it off?"

Of course, it was Carla who asked. All that Carla knew was that if something hurt, the doctors cut it off. Sometimes, Connie would catch her peering up her empty sleeve, as if she was waiting for the arm to grow back, as if she was a starfish who could make the missing part regenerate.

"No," said Connie, "but he will have to wear a cast for a long time. So my son would like me to come down there and keep Joey company and tell him stories just like the ones I tell you. So you won't see me for a while."

"Will you come back?" Jesse kept his face perfectly still but Connie could see the tears trembling at the corners of his eyes. Jesse knew about going away and never coming back.

"Yes, but it won't be for a long, long time," she said, and looked up for a moment at the supervisor, who looked away. "But let's have one more story before I have to leave. What would you like to hear?"

"I want to hear about your horse. Did you ever go riding on him?" Jason asked, and Connie reached out to pull his wheelchair closer.

"Lightning and I would go riding every morning when the dew was still on the grass. I would throw an old blanket on his strong back and slip the bit between his white teeth and off we would go. I would grip his sides very tightly with my legs and he would run very fast. Sometimes, I would close my eyes and pretend I was flying."

Jason closed his eyes and Connie could see he was pretending to feel the wind and the movement, his fingers curled around the imaginary brown leather reins.

"We would ride all morning," she continued, her voice growing softer, "while the sun would melt away the dew and warm the grass until I found the place where the strawberries were ripening. I'd pick a handful for my breakfast, while at a nearby stream Lightning would drink the water, scaring away the tadpoles swimming just below the surface."

The children grew very still, their eyes closed as they imagined the water sparkling in the sunlight and the snorting sound Lightning made when a tadpole tickled his nose.

Connie looked at their pale faces and then closed her eyes as well, willing herself to join them.

"And sometimes," she said softly, "I would see the eagles, gliding on the breeze," and for a moment, Connie too could feel the sun and see those wings outlined against the summer sky.

Exit Row

"Are you *sure* this is our row?"

Damn it! Why is she stopping now? We've already covered this!

Even though while waiting to board he had already explained numerous times which row and seat was hers—19C—she still seemed unable to remember the simple letter/number combination. And now his wife was effectively bottlenecking the already slow-moving line of passengers, first stopping to peer at the small metal label above the seats and then waiting as though it would light up in response to her question: green for yes or red for no.

"Yes," tightly. "Just look at your boarding pass."

"What?"

"Look. At. Your. Boarding. Pass," each word given its own weight. Was she deaf? Stupid? Or just pretending to be either one?

"My glasses... Where did I put my glasses? You *know* I can't see without them." She dropped her overloaded knitting bag onto an empty seat and then rummaged in her handbag, sending half-eaten rolls of mints and scraps of shopping lists cascading out of its gaping mouth to land on the aisle floor.

He looked anywhere but at what she was doing because he just couldn't bear to watch, to be a witness to her consummate stupidity. But when someone behind him pushed none too gently at his back, he knew he had to act.

"Give it to me." He grabbed for her other hand—the one clutching the now slightly damp slip—but she kept it just beyond his grasp.

Then, "There they are!" and she held her bifocals aloft in triumph. Slipping them on, she scanned the writing. "19C. Now, what seat is this?" And once again, she looked at the identifying marker as though it might have changed in the last thirty seconds. "19C! Imagine that! I stopped right at my row without even trying!" and she smiled at him, inviting him to acknowledge her success. But he looked away.

"If everyone will please move out of the aisle and into their seat, we can finish boarding."

He heard the flight attendant's command (couched as a request, to be sure, but he knew it was still an order and one solely directed at the pair of them) and tried to push past her to gain his window seat. But she sat down, piling her cracked leather purse and quilted satchel on her lap before stretching her legs in front of her.

"It feels good to sit down," and she smiled again. And she kept on smiling as he tripped over her varicose-veined extremities to fall into the window seat, the armrest bruising his hip.

"You *could* have waited. You *could* have let me go in ahead of you."

She shook her head. "Oh, no, she wanted us to sit down as quickly as possible. If I would have waited, all those people" gesturing to the passengers filing past them "would still be standing there. And that would have been so rude."

Or you could've paid attention, remembered which row was yours, let me sit down first, and then taken your seat like a normal person, he wanted to answer. But what was the point? She would have an irritatingly stupid answer that would lead to an interminably long conversation by the end of which all he would want to do was wrap his fingers around her fat, wrinkled throat and strangle her.

Sometimes, the idea was almost more attractive than he could withstand. A narrow prison cell—hell, death itself!—seemed a small price to pay just to shut her up.

But once again, self-control won out. He blocked out her voice, her presence, her very existence, as well as he could, and opened *The Times*, determined to lose himself in the business section and its latest round of stories about financial institutions brought down by investors filing class action suits.

There should be a class action suit that husbands could file against their wives, he thought, snapping the paper open before halving it neatly along its vertical fold, *when the women fail to perform as expected.*

For a moment, he lost himself in the fantasy of his wife on trial for all her misdeeds: years of charred pot roasts, favorite shirts marred with bleach stains, beloved books that unaccountably could not be found right after she cleaned the house.

"I don't understand how it could have happened," she would answer when he pointed out the issues, as though someone else might have done the damage.

At first, he would remind her that she was the one doing the cooking, the washing, and the cleaning, but the same bewildered, uncomprehending expression remained on her face. Gradually, he had come to suspect that she had known the answer all along and simply engaged him in this familiar frustrating conversation just to push him closer to the edge. But try as she might, he wouldn't go over.

No. He had no intention of letting her win. Even if it killed him.

Instead, he gave up trying to reason with her, to prove that she was at fault, or to get her to admit to the responsibility. Eventually it would all be over, he told himself. She would die and he could live what was left of his life without losing his mind. Although there were times when he wondered if years of close proximity had already damaged it beyond repair.

"All carry-on items must be stowed under the seat in front of you or in the overhead bin." The familiar singsong refrain was louder because the flight attendant was standing right beside them.

"Your bags," teeth gritted as he elbowed her. "Take care of your bags."

"Oh, yes, of course. Now, before I put them away, what will I need?"

Once again, she delved into the cavernous mouth of her handbag, an act that resembled not so much an investigation of its contents as an exercise in dumpster-diving. She pulled out a small but solid hardbound book, her over-sized cosmetic case, and a slightly brown banana whose flesh was oozing out between the slits in the peel. Then she zipped the bag closed.

"There. That should be enough for the flight." She dumped the loose items and the other bag onto his lap before shoving her purse under the seat in front of her.

The spine of the book dug into his thighs, and he tried to shift it to no avail. Then he heard, "Sir, I am going to have to ask you to place the other bag in the overhead bin, please."

The "please" was a mere formality. The flight attendant's frown made it quite clear that it was an order, not a request, and one made with what was left of her patience.

"Sit *back*," he muttered, and when his wife finally heard him, stopped fiddling with her purse, and sat back, he threw her items and quilted sack onto her lap.

"But I can't put it up there!" She looked at him in surprise. "You know I can't lift my arms that high! I have arthritis," in a confiding tone to the flight attendant who was still standing there, her black-heeled shoe tapping an impatient refrain. "And besides," in triumph, turning back to him, "I'm too short."

"Sir" but he didn't even wait for the rest of the sentence, just got to his feet and tried to maneuver past his wife. But as his right leg crossed hers, she moved just enough to trip him, sending him half-falling into the aisle.

"Stay *still!*" He regained his balance and then, grabbing the knitting bag full of skeins of yarn and crumpled patterns, started to open the overhead compartment door above them, but the flight attendant stopped him.

"That one is full, sir. These are all full."

Was it his imagination or did the attendant seem to take a perverse pleasure in denying him use of those bins that were in closest proximity to his seat?

"You'll have to go further back and see if you can find one that still has some space."

While you do exactly what, bitch? he wanted to ask, but there was no point in insulting her, even if it was her job to take care of passengers, not make their lives harder. Instead, he got a firmer grip on the cloth handles and moved down the aisle, past the rows of passengers who were already seated and waiting for take-off, which was now being delayed because he had to deal with this damned thing.

"We will be closing the cabin doors and taking off as soon as *everyone* has taken their seats," as though there were other passengers besides him still standing, still walking, still trying to find somewhere— anywhere!—to shove their damned belongings.

Finally, all the way in the rear, he found an open space into which he managed to wedge the bag before making the long walk back to row nineteen.

What would happen if I kept on walking? What if I walked right past our row, past the flight attendant, past everyone else who had the misfortune to be on this damned plane and went right out of the door, up the jetway and into the terminal? If I walked really quickly, she would never be able to find me.

For a moment, he lost himself in the fantasy: leaving the building, getting into his car, turning the key in the ignition and then driving away somewhere, anywhere, as fast as he could until it all disappeared behind him.

"Sir. Please take your seat."

He realized that he was at his row where he was doomed to stay for the next four hours, and sighing, began the process of regaining his window seat. This time, however, he was ready for her. And when she shifted her leg again, his grip on the seat back in front of him stopped him from falling forward and banging his head against the window.

A small victory, but a victory nonetheless.

"Now if you will all please pay attention..." and the familiar directions began: how to fasten the seat belt, what to do in the event of a water landing or loss of cabin pressure—all those instructions and warnings that were intended to prevent disaster or, if it should occur, to lessen its impact.

Too bad the wedding ceremony didn't come with that information, he thought. He tried to recall the day they were married, but it had taken place more than five decades ago and the exact details were lost to time. Had he even wanted to marry her? Or was it just what one did back then: get married, raise a family, and live happily ever after?

He had done the first item but it was a downhill slide after that. No kids (not that, in retrospect, he would have wanted any tangible reminder of those far-from-pleasurable twice-monthly couplings) and a job he hated in her father's company. "But Daddy has already planned it!" she had told him and, even in those early days, he recognized when he was up against an immovable force and so acquiesced. And then, year after year of steadily increasing aggravations that wore him down like water dripping on a rock.

A bump—he hadn't realized that the plane had started down the runway in preparation for take-off.

"Sir. Your seat belt."

He flushed and fastened himself in, not meeting the flight attendant's eyes. Then, "*Mine* is fastened," his wife pointed out happily, like a little kid waiting for praise, and she got what she wanted.

"Yes, I can see that. Thank you for following our rules. If *everyone* did that," pointedly, "flights would be so much smoother."

He turned his head away to look out the window. But the darkness outside combined with the lit interior of the plane turned the glass into a mirror, and he saw—or did he just imagine it?—the two exchanging conspiratorial smiles.

Damn them. Damn all women, he thought while the tightness in his chest constricted his breathing. He took some deep breaths, trying to calm down, hoping stress would release its iron grip. That was all it was—just stress. He was sure of it, regardless of what the doctor had said.

"If you feel pain, just put one of these under your tongue," the cardiologist had said at the last appointment, holding the tiny bottle aloft. "And seek immediate medical attention, of course."

"I'll make sure he does," his wife had said, and the doctor had first smiled at her and then gave him a look that said how lucky he was to have someone watching out for him.

A few more breaths, and now he was calmer and in less pain. Maybe if he read the paper page by page, article by article, line by line, it might last until they touched down in Phoenix.

The trip was her idea. She said she had always wanted to go to Phoenix. Why, he didn't know and didn't even bother to ask since her answer was bound to make little sense anyway. He had long since given up trying to understand the inner workings of her mind. All he knew was that he had come home from the barbershop to find the itinerary on the table and her bag half-packed.

"It will be a lovely trip. The weather is so much nicer there than here," and she gestured to the window, where the sleet was needling the glass unmercifully.

But all that meant was that for a solid week he would be chained to her side, either stuck in the small hotel room or trapped in a tour bus. Each year since he retired, they took a trip, and each year she picked the destination, bought the tickets, and then gave him the itinerary: a *fait accompli*.

And each year, he suffered through those seven days, hating not so much the scenery or sites as her proximity. At least at home, he could escape—play golf once a week, mow the lawn, or when the snow piled up, shovel the drive. It didn't matter what he did as long as she wasn't a part of it. And it worked— for fifty-one weeks. But the fifty-second was when he lost his freedom and instead became part of a two-man chain gang.

He turned the page of the newspaper, hoping to find something that would capture his attention, and then realized that some pages were missing.

"What happened to the paper?" he asked aloud, not expecting an answer, but she replied.

"Oh, I needed something to wrap the fish bones in before I threw them away. I didn't think you'd mind," although she knew damned well he *would* mind, that the paper had been neatly folded and slipped inside the outside pocket of his carry-on so it would be ready for the trip. She knew it and took it anyway—and then folded it back up so he wouldn't notice until it was too late to buy another.

He wanted to explode at her, beat her over the head with what was left of the paper, but instead he breathed in and out as slowly as possible, trying to get his anger under control. He wouldn't give in. Not yet. Not when there were so many witnesses. Not when they were in this sardine can thirty-five-thousand feet above the surface of the earth. Not when he couldn't escape, cleanly, quickly, permanently.

He shoved the paper into the seat pocket and then looked out the window. But the white clouds obscured any view of the world below. Not that, at this hour, there would be much to see. She always chose the latest possible flight, and this one was no different, not departing until ten at night.

"When we land, it'll be two hours earlier," she explained. "And the flight was so much cheaper."

Although it would *still* be late at night, he thought, and by the time they got to the hotel room, he would be so tired he wouldn't be able to sleep. She, on the other hand, would immediately start snoring as soon as her head hit the pillow and then wake up bright and early the next morning, fully refreshed and ready to go.

Not for the first time he wondered why he allowed himself to be dragged on these vacations every year. Why didn't he just cancel the tickets or, better yet, cancel *his* and let her go alone? After all these years, was he just incapable of fighting the immovable force that was his wife?

The thought was disturbing, unsettling. He needed something to distract his mind, to wipe out that mental image of himself being dragged by invisible chains along a path of her devising that led inexorably to his death.

He checked the seat pocket, hoping for an inflight magazine, but she had already captured the sole issue for their row. Not that she was reading it. No, she was engaged in her book, some trashy novel she had picked up in the terminal, licking the tips of her fingers each time she had to turn a page. As for the magazine, it was wedged between her ample hip and the armrest. He'd have to reach across her to get to it but that would bring him far closer to her body than he wanted.

Maybe he could sleep. He slipped off his jacket and balled it up to put between his head and the window and then, angling his body away from her, he closed his eyes. If he slept, he could at least forget for those few hours that she was next to him. Lord knows, that strategy worked for years in their marital bed.

Breathe in, breathe out, relax, relax... He silently repeated the mantra, the only useful tool he was able to gain from a Discovery Channel show on relaxation. He might have learned more if she hadn't picked that moment to run the vacuum cleaner in the living room. Slowly he felt the tension in his neck subside, his heartbeat slow, and his muscles soften. He had just reached the point of dozing off when a light pierced his closed eyelids.

"Mine wasn't bright enough," she said, when he turned to look at her, "so I had to turn yours on, too," and she smiled.

He should have brought an eye mask to block out the light. He should have brought earplugs, too, so he wouldn't have had to hear her either. He should have brought an eye mask, earplugs and some undetectable but lethal poison to drop into her food so she would go into convulsions and die before the plane could land.

But he hadn't, and now he was forced to sit there and listen to her chatter on about the story she was reading—some stupid gothic romance that was a ludicrous choice for a woman her age, anyway.

"We'll start the refreshment service in a few moments."

The announcement was a welcome one, not because he was hungry or thirsty but because he could count on her to want to eat and drink. And while her mouth was occupied, she wouldn't be able to talk.

He didn't want anything, though. The hamburger he had eaten at one of the airport's overpriced fast food places was sitting rocklike in his stomach, and even now he could feel the stomach acid eating a hole in his internal lining. It would have been all right if he had taken his antacid pills, the ones he always made sure to slip into his jacket pocket, but he hadn't. Not because he forgot but because they weren't there. He realized that when he searched in vain for the bottle.

"Oh, that bottle?" she had said, after watching him check both pockets. "I think I saw it fall out when you took your jacket out of the bin at security. Yes, that is exactly what happened," triumphantly, as though he was supposed to be pleased that she knew where he had lost the bottle. "It fell out of your pocket and I picked it up and set it off to one side and then, oh, my, I guess I forgot to take it when we left. Did you need it?"

A stupid question because she *knew* he needed it. He took a pill before each meal, and sometimes, if the day had been stressful or she had been particularly aggravating, one more at night.

Now he wouldn't be able to take any at all. And since it was his last refill, he would have to wait until he got home and scheduled a doctor's appointment to get any more. In the meantime, the burning would go on and on and on.

Like her voice. Like her existence.

"Now what can I get you?"

He turned to answer the flight attendant, but realized she was speaking, not to him but to his wife, who was engaged in a long drawn-out process of making her selection from the paltry choices: peanuts or cookies, coffee or tea, juice or water.

"Well, let's see," and she mulled over the options.

How could she be hungry? It wasn't as though she hadn't eaten! She had already ingested quite a lot: the six-dollar cheeseburger and fries at Burger Boy and then, less than an hour later, a peanut butter sandwich, candy bar, and the twin to the leaking banana—all pulled from the stockpile in her handbag while they were waiting to board.

It was embarrassing to see her bring all that food into the airport, but what was even more disgusting was the *way* she ate: taking great bites from the sandwich and then turning to talk to him, her mouth still full with bits of peanut butter caught in the corners.

It was disgusting and yet she did it, like all the other things she did that humiliated him when they were in public.

"Take your time," the flight attendant said, and of course, she did, finally deciding on both peanuts *and* cookies, coffee *and* juice.

"And you?" The attendant's *Can't you hurry up and make a choice already?* tone was a sharp contrast to the one she had employed with his wife.

"Nothing" he answered, and the woman turned to the people across the aisle with an audible sniff, as though resenting the seconds she spent asking her question when he wasn't planning on having anything anyway.

"But the snacks are free!" his wife said, as though he was an imbecile who had never flown before. 'Why don't you take one? Here," and she pushed the opened bag of peanuts at him, spilling half of its contents on his lap in the process. "Have a few."

"You *know* I am allergic to peanuts."

"Oh, that's right. I forgot. Cookie then?" and she smiled again.

He didn't even bother to answer but turned away, checking his watch to see how much longer this flight would last. At least two more hours before they touched down. Two more hours of being trapped next to this thing that was his wife. Two more hours of watching her and the flight attendant collude against him. Right now, he had no doubt that if he asked for medical aid, even *that* wouldn't be forthcoming. How did his wife manage to get everyone on her side? He didn't even *do* anything and they were already against him.

He rested his perspiring head against the cold window and tried to slow his breathing again while ignoring the burning in his stomach. But both efforts were unsuccessful. Two hours. One hundred twenty minutes. Or a lifetime, depending on how you looked at it.

"Mmm," and she nudged him sharply with her elbow. "This is so good. You really should have had something. He should have had something," turning to the people across the aisle. "You know, my husband has stomach issues," lowering her voice as though she were talking about some embarrassing disease, "and if he goes without eating, he gets an awful burning and sometimes even diarrhea."

"Oh, for God's sakes," but nothing could stop her now. She would go on, recounting every ache and pain, illness, and injury he had suffered since their marriage while he sat there, red-faced and tried to pretend that he was anywhere but there.

"Will you just eat, please!" and she turned back to him, smiling.

"Of course! Actually," as she dumped the contents of the six sugar packets into the foam cup, "I think I want to drink the—oh, my!" and somehow the scalding hot coffee sloshed over the edge and right onto his lap, seeping through the polyester material to burn the tender flesh of his inner thigh.

"Damn it!" he exploded and then magically the flight attendant was there. But not to offer help—he realized that when she said "Sir! Your language, please!" without even so much as giving him a napkin to sop up the liquid. "There are children present!" as though they hadn't heard the same words from their own parents, he thought angrily.

Then, "Can I get you another cup?" to his wife, as though the bitch deserved one after being so careless.

Or was it really carelessness? Sometimes, when things liked this happened—the dinner knife that she knocked onto his lap where it just missed his balls, the hot water tank set at a scalding temperature in time for his nightly shower, the juice she gave him from a pitcher that had been sitting on the counter for hours—he wondered if she wasn't trying to kill him.

"Let me up," and he grabbed what was left of her snacks off her tray and tossed them onto her lap, while shoving her juice and now empty coffee cup at the attendant. "Let me up" even louder, and he shoved the tray up out of the way, and then, without even waiting for her to move her legs, stepped over her, pushing the attendant out of his way as he headed down the aisle.

He'd go to the restroom, cool the burn with some water and then—what? Could he possibly stay in that narrow cubicle until it was time for the plane to begin its descent? And would that be so bad? He would at least have a place to sit in peace and quiet.

No, he realized. If he tried that, that damned flight attendant was bound to beat on the door and everyone would turn to watch him exit the bathroom. He needed another strategy, another way of avoiding her for at least the balance of the flight. And miracle of miracles, one presented itself as he was heading back to his seat.

There, just a few rows behind her, an empty aisle seat. *I'll just sit there*, he thought, and suited action to idea. The passenger to his left glanced up and then quickly looked away. *He's afraid of me*, he thought with satisfaction. *And well he should be. No one knows what I'm capable of, what I can do if I'm pushed beyond my limit!*

And he had been—not just with what happened on this flight but for all those years that led up to it. He really couldn't take any more. He just couldn't.

He could feel his heart begin its erratic rhythm and a cold sweat beading on his forehead.

He'd had enough. One more minute of this life with her and he would explode. And now his heart was pounding and, from a distance, he could see his fingers clenching the armrest. He ought to take a nitro pill. If he didn't, the pain would get worse and his heart would beat harder.

But his pills were in the breast pocket of his jacket and his jacket was up there. With her.

"Sir. This isn't your seat. You can't sit here" but he couldn't look at the flight attendant. Not now. He was too busy trying to breathe past the increasing tightness.

"Sir, I am going to have to insist that you return to your seat immediately!"

But *that* wasn't going to be an option, because, even if he *wanted* to—and God knows he didn't!— for some reason his leg muscles wouldn't have obeyed his brain's commands. And now the pain was even worse and he knew—he knew!—that even if he took a pill, it wouldn't help. And did he want one, really?

"Sir! You can't sit here. It's not your seat. Yours is a few rows up. This is the exit row."

Exit row.

The pain was unbearable but he mustered just enough energy to answer, "Thank God" before closing his eyes and letting the pain take him away.

Waiting for Sara

"Mom, it's Sara."

Her voice was distorted by the miles of wire separating us—how many miles I could only guess.

"Where are you?"

So many of our conversations began like that, with Sara making contact, and me desperately trying to keep that contact alive, sending out my love like a rope to bind her to me.

"Things haven't been goin' too good here." Her voice was slurred. Alcohol? Drugs? I couldn't tell.

"Sara." My voice sharpened with worry. "Tell me where you are. Are you okay?"

"Cool, Ma." Her voice faded away, and then came back again. "So what's happenin'?"

"I'd love to see you, Sara. Tell me where you are, and I'll come get you. Or give me your number and I'll call you back."

The phone company could trace a number, I thought. I'll tell them it's an emergency. I'll tell them we were cut off. We *were* cut off. Between my daughter and me, there was a chasm deeper than the Great Divide. And every spar I threw across fell to the bottom, the echoes endlessly crashing through my life.

"So, look, I gotta go." There were sounds in the background—doors slamming and voices raised in anger. "But, hey, it's been great, y'know," and then the line was dead.

I didn't want to put the receiver down, even when the buzzing was replaced by the recorded voice asking me to "please hang up now."

Finally, I replaced it on the cradle—gently, the way you close a door when the baby is sleeping and all you wanted to do was peek inside without awakening her.

When Sara was a baby, I used to open and close her door a hundred times, afraid that if I missed checking her every fifteen minutes, she would die. Crib death was my big fear then, followed by child molesters and kidnappers as she grew older.

I hated seeing those pictures on milk cartons—smiling faces snapped in their school-picture pose, with the plaintive cry "Have you seen this child?" emblazoned below. I didn't want to be reminded of what could happen to any child—my child—despite a mother's careful concern.

Now, I wanted to take her high school graduation picture and send it to Sara, pleading, "Have you seen my daughter? Please bring her back."

It has been at least four years since we lived together. One cold November morning, she packed her clothes, her favorite stuffed bear, and the small stash of marijuana she thought I didn't know about into the suitcase I had given her for her eighteenth birthday, and left. Just like that. I had no warning, no way to prepare.

Well, no, that isn't strictly true. A blind person could have seen it coming—the logical culmination of shouted words and slammed doors, of hostile stares and muttered phrases.

A blind person, yes, but not a mother. Past experience with a two-year-old's tantrums was little preparation for a teenager's rebellion or an adult child's rejection.

Sara's thirteenth birthday had marked the beginning of battles between us, leaving me bewildered, hurt, and angry—sometimes all at the same time.

"But why can't I go?" Sara's voice was shrill, carrying through walls into the kitchen, where I was peeling potatoes for dinner. That was her job, but it seemed easier to do it myself rather than argue with her. Lately, quarrels had become the only form of communication between my teenaged daughter and me.

"You're only in junior high. You're too young to go to a concert. It's dangerous. People get crazy at those things!"

"Well, it's stupid!" She flounced into the room, wearing a skirt that was far too short. I had told her any number of times to let the hem down, that it was verging on indecent. But she wouldn't listen. "Everybody is going—all my friends! You just don't want me to have any fun! I hate you!" screaming the last words as she slammed the front door behind her.

The knife slipped on the potato skin and sliced my finger. I watched the blood well up through the tears in my eyes and tried very hard not to let her words cut my heart. All the parenting books said that this was a typical teenage stage and not to take it personally.

Good advice. If only I could follow it.

She didn't come home that night. Instead, she slept at her girlfriend's house, while I paced the floor and debated calling the police. In the end, I simply waited for her—the way I had waited for her to be born.

Overdue, yet stubbornly refusing to cooperate with nature, Sara was born by cesarean section. At the time, I thought it was my body that refused to surrender this new life without a fight. But perhaps it was Sara herself who was not ready to be born. Did she somehow know how difficult life would be? Was she trying to hold off accepting the responsibility for her own existence?

In the recovery room, I had marveled at her body, counting fingers and toes over and over again, rejoicing in the reality of her presence. I pictured us functioning as a single unit—mother-and-daughter—sharing joys and happiness in a peaceful home.

Not surprisingly, reality was different.

"Mommy, I'm bored."

My daughter twined her six-year-old arms around my neck, pulling me away from the desk and the bills awaiting payment. There was so much to take care of: grocery shopping and house cleaning, meals to cook and clothes to wash. And Sara.

Sometimes, I would wonder what I could have accomplished if I hadn't had been a single parent. Sometimes, I would envy my childless friends who moved unencumbered through life, achieving goal after goal.

Most of the time, I would try not to think of what might have been and instead, would take pleasure in brushing Sara's hair or listening to her sing to her stuffed bear. Most of the time, I would try to remember what a blessing children could be, and how many infertile women wept sterile tears.

Most of the time, I would succeed.

"Sara, Mommy's working. Please go watch television." If I had more money, I could hire a sitter, carve out some alone time to get caught up. But Sara and I were barely able to exist on my secretarial income. There was no extra money to pay for the luxury of solitude.

"But, Mommy, you promised we could go to the park today." Her fingers pulled at my hair as her words pulled at my mind.

"In a minute," I said, adding sharply, "Now go in the other room and leave me alone!"

Years later, I can still feel her arms slipping free of my neck.

When Sara first moved out, I felt disoriented, like returning to a room and discovering that it was not the same as when I had left it a moment ago. Nothing anyone said—and they all tried to say something appropriate from "She'll come around someday" to "You did the best you could"—was of any use to me.

No mother ever believes she has done her best. Her memories are filled with moments when words rise unbidden from somewhere deep inside, fueled by frustration and anger. Words spoken to hurt the one she loved the most. The wrong words that can never be recalled.

"Mom."

I didn't recognize her in the darkness. The landlord had promised to replace the light bulb on the landing, but somehow, he had never gotten around to it. So I carried a torch to light my way.

"Sara?" I turned the wavering beam towards the small figure near the stairs.

I knew it was my daughter, and yet, so much was different. I hadn't seen her in nearly six months. She had dyed her hair shoe-polish black and wore it pulled back from her thin face, looking so much older than her nineteen years.

I remember how I used to braid her golden brown hair into one long plait. It was so thick that the elastic band could wrap around it only twice, and the curls kept slipping free to twist with a life of their own around her neck.

"Could I come inside?"

I realized that I had been staring at her, but not really seeing her. I was seeing instead my little girl, not this unhappy stranger with torn jeans, holding a dirty denim jacket smelling of cigarettes and worse.

"Yes, of course," and it wasn't until she passed by me to enter the apartment that I saw the tattoo on her shoulder—a small spider web with a fly caught in the center.

"I'm having a baby. And don't lecture," she added, holding up a hand to try to forestall my words. But she was too late.

"A baby? Are you crazy? Don't you practice safe sex? What about AIDS? And who's the father? Do you even know who he is? How could you do this?"

I knew, as soon as the words left my mouth, that it was wrong, all wrong—that all I was doing was driving her away. But I couldn't stop. "I suppose you want me to help you get out of this mess, just like always. I don't hear from you for weeks on end until you want something. When are you going to take some responsibility for your life?"

"I don't want anything from you. I can do this on my own. I just thought you'd want to know!" She pulled on her coat. "I'm leaving. I knew this was a mistake."

"Sara, wait!" but the door slammed on my words.

I knew that the issues I raised were valid and legitimate, but that was cold comfort. My response certainly didn't help the situation. What I should have done was keep quiet and let her talk, and then try to reach out to her.

When I wasn't being confronted by her, I could be reasonable, compassionate, understanding. But when she was there before me, all the anger stored up inside me poured out in a torrent of thoughtless words.

Maybe it wasn't really anger but pain. Maybe, deep inside, I hated the fact that she had the power to hurt me and so I tried to hurt her in return.

After that visit, she stayed out of touch for several weeks while I tried to come to terms with the news, wondering if she would be okay, if the baby would be born healthy, if they would both come home so we could start afresh. But a late-night call ended the fruitless speculations.

"Mom, I'm in the hospital. I lost the baby."

"What happened? Are you all right?" I pulled my sweatpants on over my pajamas and then rummaged for my keys amid the clutter on my nightstand.

"I'm fine. I don't know. It just happened."

There was a note I recognized in her voice—defiance and fear wrapped up into one. She'd been doing drugs—even without clear evidence, I knew my suspicions were correct. A mother's sixth sense, I suppose. Maybe that was what had caused the miscarriage. Or perhaps God had intervened, not willing to subject an innocent child to an unprepared new mother and a grandmother who had obviously failed the first time around.

"Where are you? I'll be right there."

"I don't want you to come. I'll be out tomorrow. They had to give me some blood, but I'll be okay. I just thought I'd let you know."

That was it. The connection was broken. I sat on the edge of my bed, rumpled sheets bunched behind me, and looked at the notes I had been making before I had fallen asleep.

Call the obstetrician. Find out about prenatal classes. Clean out spare bedroom.

I threw the notes away. I didn't need them anymore.

Life went back to normal, so to speak. I didn't see Sara—she had left town without giving me a forwarding address.

"I'll write you when I get a place" was the message she had left on my answering machine. No mention of which direction she was heading, no indication which part of the country she was running to. All I knew was that she was running away—away from me, and, I suppose, away from all the decisions she had made so far.

She ran for a long time—almost a year.

"Mom."

I was groggy with sleep, having gone to bed too late the night before. The clock read 4:30, and it took me a minute to understand who was calling me at that ungodly hour.

"Sara?"

"Mom, I just called to tell you that I'm in L.A. with some friends."

Los Angeles? Friends? Whom does she know across the country from us?

"I'll call you when I get back. Okay?"

"Sara, wait!" but she had hung up before the words could travel the long distance from the East Coast to the West. It was two years before I heard from her again.

When there is silence between us, I am overcome with grief for her—for the choices she has made, for the life she is living. Late into the night, I lie awake and wonder at which point she had missed the path, and whether I could have brought her back if I had paid more attention, been more attuned to her needs.

They say we are responsible for our own lives. They say that, despite the best love and attention, some children will stray, and that parents should not accept blame for decisions their offspring make. They say that sometimes, the best we can do is to give them time.

Time. I do not give her time so much as surrender it to her, fighting tooth and nail to stop the slow progression of days and nights when Sara is someplace unknown to me.

Since that last call I am, once again, waiting, passing time until Sara calls again. I have to hope I'll hear from her; that one night, the phone will ring, and Sara will be there. It's hope that keeps me from changing her bedroom into a work room, that makes me buy her favorite cereal to replace the one in the pantry, six months old and still unopened.

Some nights, I plan the conversation: neutral, non-critical, supportive. "I'm glad you called. I've missed you. Will you be coming back soon? Are you okay?"

Some nights, I remind myself that she is basically an intelligent person, and many other young adults make a string of bad choices before getting a handle on life.

Some nights, I look at her baby pictures and cry.

But I am always waiting for Sara.

Beautiful Dreamer

"Eleanor, Eleanor... you look beautiful tonight."

The words drifted into her mind, like leaves in an autumn breeze, settling softly in the forefront of her consciousness. She awoke to find the phone cradled between her cheek and the pillow, the insistent buzzing the only sound from the black receiver.

Had there been a voice on the line? Or had she only dreamed it?

She had had dreams before—the kind that would wake her like an alarm bell. Heart pounding, pulse racing, it would take her several moments to get her bearings and know where she was and that she had been dreaming.

Sometimes, her mouth would be dry and her throat sore, as though she had carried on a long conversation with someone now absent. But she always knew when she had been sleeping. However real the dreams would seem—and at times, the line between reality and dreamland was very fine indeed—she always knew the difference.

She was certain this had not been a dream.

And yet, no one had ever called Eleanor on the telephone. No one had ever told her she looked beautiful. No one talked to her at all—not to the real Eleanor, the one hiding behind the straight dull-brown hair, the plain face. They only talked to Eleanor-the-tenant, Eleanor-the-secretary, Eleanor-the-faceless-person amid thousands of other faceless people of the city.

But now someone had seen her. Someone called her by name and told her she was beautiful. With that single phone call, everything had changed.

"Good morning, Miss," said the flower seller as he did every day for the past five years when Eleanor passed his cart on her way to the bus stop.

Usually, she nodded in return, or mumbled a fast "'morning" as she passed him. She didn't like talking to strangers, and although they had seen each other for half a decade, he was a stranger still.

But this time, she stopped and smiled at him.

"How are you?" she asked, and, without waiting for an answer went on talking. "Isn't it a lovely day?"

He looked up at the sky, overcast and promising rain.

"Oh, it's a wonderful day!" she rushed on. "My goodness, there's my bus!" and she dashed to the stop, the few beginning drops of rain hardly halting her flight.

"A lovely day," she repeated to the doorman of the building where she worked. "A perfectly marvelous morning," to the receptionist, busy answering the phone and routing calls.

Her enthusiasm lasted until lunchtime, fading only when no one came forward to talk to her, to tell her how beautiful she looked that day, to apologize, perhaps, for the late-night phone call.

Today would be no different at all, she realized. It was just as if nothing had ever happened.

Perhaps it didn't, Eleanor told herself, and rubbed her temples as she felt the familiar ache. She knew from experience that, by five p.m., her head would be throbbing, and she would hardly be able to see. The doctor had said it was nerves and stress and had given her some pink pills to take. But they didn't seem to help.

By nightfall, Eleanor could hardly stand the pain. She crawled into her bed, pulling the thin cover over her, and prayed for rest, for sleep, for total oblivion. And when she awoke sometime deep in the night, her first thought was how wonderful it felt to be able to move her head without pain.

But what was she holding?

The receiver was warm. She must have been clutching it for some time. And the echoes of words remained, caught between her mind and the pillow.

"You are so beautiful, Eleanor. You are what any man would want. *I* want you, Eleanor."

She shook her head to clear away the last vestiges of sleep and set the phone back on the hook.

Who was calling her so late, so very late, in the night? Who believed her to be every man's dream?

The next morning, Eleanor found herself making small but foolish mistakes. She added sugar to her coffee cup, only to repeat the same action a few moments later. She forced herself to drink the sickeningly sweet liquid as a penance for her error.

"I need to concentrate on what I'm doing," she admonished herself, speaking the words aloud. Eleanor frequently talked to herself. If she hadn't, the apartment would be as silent as a tomb.

As for being forgetful, it had happened before. She had left stores carrying merchandise and only her general air of bewilderment and surprise prevented the manager from charging her with shoplifting. Often, after work, she would arrive at her front door, only to find it unlocked and open since her morning departure.

Sometimes, she would be so lost in her thoughts that she would travel the streets of the city, oblivious to her surroundings.

But never had she heard voices, save her own and the ones belonging to real people in the real world.

"He must be real—a real person," she whispered. In the mirror, she saw, not a lonely woman, but a beautiful young girl—every man's dream, every man's desire.

"He will call again," and with that hope worn like a shield, she went out into daylight.

But as days passed, the secret lover was determinedly absent from her life. Each morning, Eleanor would awaken and wonder, "Will he call today? Will I see him somewhere—in a crowd, on a bus, by my apartment door when I come home—and our eyes will meet and we will touch?"

She could hardly bear the suspense. She had taken to going straight home from work instead of lingering at shop windows in case he phoned again, but the telephone stubbornly refused to make a sound.

Perhaps it was over, she thought hopelessly. Memories of other stillborn romances moved through her mind as past hurts and long-buried desires ached within her. She was not so old, she thought resentfully, that her life should be only memories and empty ones at that. Surely she was entitled to one love affair.

A month after the calls began, Eleanor was plagued once again with a headache, the worst she had ever felt. Barely able to function, she suffered through the long workday. At day's end, she gratefully took her place on the bus heading home, resting her cheek against the grimy window, thinking only of her bed and soft pillow.

And those little pink pills. Maybe she would try them again. Take four or six, instead of the two prescribed. Eight or ten—what did it matter, after all? All she wanted was for the pain to stop.

Almost blacking out from the pain (Had it ever been this bad before?), she found herself at home, in her bed, with no real memory of how she had gotten there or if she had passed anyone on the way.

"Sleep," she moaned, not bothering to take off her shoes or slip her dress from her narrow shoulders. She closed her eyes, fighting the waves of pain, and dropped quickly into oblivion, her breath so faint that her chest barely moved. But behind her closed lids, her eyes shifted erratically, following dream visions more real than the life she lived.

By morning the pain was gone, but so was her hope.

"There is no mystery lover," she told herself as she drank her cold coffee. (Had she forgotten to warm it or had it just sat there on the counter so long that the heat had dissipated?) "He'll not call again, I'll never see him, it's over. It never even began."

She wondered if those little pink pills could stop the pain of an aching heart. Could they obliterate the sense of loss and longing that plagued her? Perhaps tonight she would try them, she thought, as she closed the door behind her. Perhaps it was time to give up, give in, she decided on her way to the bus stop. No one would miss her anyway.

Lost in her thoughts, she would have passed the flower seller had he not called out to her.

"Your flowers, Miss," and his voice jerked her around. He was holding a sheaf of deep red roses. She could almost taste the fragrance.

"For me?" and bewildered, she held out her arms to receive the flowers.

"Yes, for you," and his impatience caught at her. Why was he angry with her? She didn't know anything about them.

"But I don't—" she started to say, when another customer called to him, and he turned, saying only "They're yours," before leaving her.

They must be from *him*, she thought. I've not gone mad—there really *is* someone and he *had* called me, and now, he's sent me roses! Maybe tonight will be the night—maybe tonight I will *see* him!

#

As she headed to the bus stop, the flower seller turned to his wife standing behind the counter and shook his head.

"That lady, she is getting stranger by the day," he said. "Last night, she was in such a mood—picked out the roses, paid me, and said to hold them 'til this morning. Now, she acts like she doesn't know anything about them. Is she crazy or what?"

"Ah, what does it matter, Fred?" answered his wife prosaically. "Crazy or not, her money is as good as anyone else's. Now, what do you want for supper?"

NANCY CHRISTIE

The Kindness of Strangers

"I have always relied on the kindness of strangers."

Mona remembered that line from a Tennessee Williams' play—*A Streetcar Named Desire*, she recalled. She had caught it once on television, although the picture was so fuzzy and indistinct that she couldn't really see the faces of the actors. But the words were clear and moving and very, very sad.

They gave her an extra dose of her medicine that night, so she would stop crying and fall asleep. And after that, they monitored her television viewing more closely.

Not that she watched television all that often. The set was old and its performance erratic. Donated to the hospital common room by the grateful family of a now-deceased patient, the failing picture screen usually broke up into wavy lines, giving the impression that you were viewing the show through a rough and choppy sea.

But at least the sound was adequate, and that was all that mattered. Mona figured she could always imagine how the characters looked: their hair, their eyes, the expressions on their faces. She had a good imagination.

But in spite of what they said (and who *they* were, even now Mona didn't know) she could distinguish fact from fiction, or reality from fantasy. Take the food, for example—the strange-tasting coffee, the sugar hiding the bitterness under the sweet.

Someone—Kate, perhaps?—said there was nothing wrong with the food. It was all part of the sickness, Kate said. It was the sickness that made Mona believe things that weren't true—terrible things, hurtful things. It was the sickness that made Mona accuse Kate of doing those horrible things.

Mona knew better. She knew there was something bad in the food that Kate was serving her. But Kate (And who *was* Kate anyway?) won and the doctors put Mona in this place to treat her for depression or delusion or some other D-word that was their explanation of the truth.

That's when Mona knew that Kate was nothing to her—no relative but a stranger, and not even a kind one. No one with an ounce of kindness would have put an old woman all alone in a place like this.

But, Mona told herself in the months that followed, she wouldn't be in here forever. She had a friend on the outside (Was that a line from a Jimmy Cagney movie? Never mind. It didn't matter.) who would get her out of this place. By herself, Mona would never get free. But with the help of the stranger-who-was-her-friend, she just might escape.

Her friend would come to visit Mona at odd times of the day and they would make plans for Mona's flight to freedom. One of the plans, later abandoned because it was too difficult to get explosives, involved blowing up the main entrance where the closed circuit monitors were stationed. Mona liked that plan, simply because she resented being watched every minute of the day and night. There was a thing called privacy, after all.

They had other plans as well. Mona's friend was a veritable storehouse of ideas. She, like Mona, had an excellent imagination. But so far they hadn't settled on which strategy to use, which wasn't helped by the fact that Mona's friend (What was her name, anyway?) could only meet with her when no one was around—"when the coast is clear," she would wisecrack. And it seemed like someone was always nearby—giving medicine, adjusting bedcovers, or checking locks.

Once, as they were planning and plotting, they were almost caught. But the jingle of the keys gave away the nurse's arrival, and Mona's friend disappeared before the door opened.

When it wasn't the nurses with their endless pills and potions, it was the doctors, hemming and hawing as they pried open her eyes and looked down her throat and touched her breasts "to listen to your heart," they always said.

And then there was Kate—mysterious Kate, ubiquitous Kate. She would come to see Mona under the pretense of caring how she was. Mona never knew when to expect her. If she did, she would do her best to hide—slide under the bed where dustballs tickled her nose, or lie in the cold porcelain tub with the mildewed shower curtain drawn around her.

Mona had told her several times that she wanted to be left alone, that she didn't want or need to see her, to just stop coming. And then Kate would pretend to cry and the nurses would shake their heads at Mona's cruelty. And later when they gave her the nightly shot, the needle would go in with an extra hard push and the injection site would be black and blue in the morning.

Mona tried to explain that Kate was nothing to her—a stranger, in fact—but no one would listen. No one except Mona's friend. But she had no authority over the doctors and nurses, and she was too afraid to confront Kate. She said Kate would hurt her and make her go away.

So it was left to Mona to weather these visits from Stranger Kate as best she could until the day she would be free of this place and return—return where? She never got that far in her plans. The drugs must have wiped clean parts of her memory because she wasn't entirely sure where she was supposed to go once the brick building with barred windows and locked doors was safely behind her.

She wanted to go home, but she didn't know where home was or if it was even still there. Kate talked about home a lot. She said that when Mona was better, she could come home.

Mona hated when Kate said that, though. She hated everything Kate said, even the way she said Mona's name. She always stumbled over it, making it sound like "mama" or some other such thing.

"My name is Mona," she had said the first time Kate mumbled, and repeated her name again, drawing out the syllables loudly, "MO—NA."

Kate had started crying then, and since that day, she had either avoided saying Mona's name or choked over it, like it was a piece of tough meat she was forced to chew.

"Here's someone to see you." The bright, determined voice of the nurse broke into Mona's thoughts, and turning her head, she saw Kate trailing behind.

Mona gave her a long look and then turned back to the television. It wasn't on, but that wasn't the point.

"I'm busy," she answered, watching the empty screen, but the nurse only walked away without comment, leaving Kate behind.

"I brought you some cookies" and Kate held out the container of oatmeal squares to Mona.

Probably poisoned, Mona thought. "Well, I don't want them. And I don't want you," she said more loudly. "Go away."

Rising from her chair, she threw the box of cookies Kate had pressed into her unwilling hands into a nearby trashcan before hastening down the hall toward her room.

Let her cry her crocodile tears, Mona thought, glancing back once to see Kate with her face buried in a tissue. *Soon, I'll be free of this place. Soon, I'll be able to go—but go where? Well, somewhere. Anywhere. All that matters is getting out of here.*

Almost stumbling over her loose slippers, Mona hurried into her room. Kate was still far down the hall, complaining, about the cookies, no doubt.

"It doesn't matter," Mona said aloud, pulling the covers from the bed and wrapping them around herself from head to toe, leaving only a tiny space by her mouth for fresh air to enter. "She can't get to me in here," and she settled down to wait for her friend to come with the latest plan of escape.

#

When the nurse returned to the television room, she asked Kate, "Where did your mother go?"

"I offered her the cookies," Kate answered, "but she threw them away. The medicine doesn't seem to be helping her at all. Sometimes I wonder if she'll ever be better."

She wiped her eyes and then smiled bleakly. "I suppose I ought to try again. She went to her room. Should I—"

"You should go home," the nurse said firmly, patting Kate on the shoulder. "You've done the best you could. No daughter could have done more than you have." Her voice was rough with sympathy and concern.

Kate pressed her hand in gratitude. Sometimes, she thought, it meant so much—the simple kindness of strangers.

Annabelle

"My father was a painter," Annabelle had said—was it at the second session or the third?—"and my mother would pose for him."

Annabelle remembered watching her father paint in the cold, clear light filtering into his studio. He used canvas and oils the way God had used clay, creating life from inanimate objects. The walls of the house were hung with his paintings—those his agent could not convince him to release—and everywhere Annabelle looked, her mother's dark eyes would follow her, glowing on the canvas.

Sometimes, after a long session in the studio, her mother would be pale and weak, barely able to stand, so colorless that one would think her a ghost. The portraits, by contrast, were pulsing with life. Annabelle had feared that her father was drawing the very lifeblood from her mother, leaving behind an empty shell.

And yet, her mother gloried in the attention, willingly changing herself into any figure her husband desired, just to be able to stand there, caught by his passion, while he painted.

His work sold quite well in galleries across the country, but even if it had not, her father would have continued to paint and her mother to pose.

And Annabelle-the-child would be standing, somewhere just outside their line of sight, watching. And waiting.

"Did your father never paint you, Anna?" Jules' question was spoken so softly in the darkened room that it almost seemed the words originated in Annabelle's mind, and she answered them just to hear her own voice echoing in the darkness.

Annabelle blushed, an ugly red stain against her pale skin. "He did not paint children," she answered hesitantly, not adding that once she had asked— begged!—her father to paint her.

She had been young, five or six, and perhaps a little jealous of the attention given her mother during those endless sessions in the studio. Just once, she wanted her father to look at her with the intensity he reserved for his wife—to fix her so clearly on the canvas that there was no possibility of her ceasing to exist.

The promises she had made—"I won't move! I won't even breathe if you would just paint me!"— were all in vain. Her father had looked at her absently, his brush suspended in mid-stroke, and Annabelle realized in that moment that he wasn't at all certain who she was or why she was there in his studio.

Her mother, with gentle, insistent fingers, had urged her reluctant daughter from the room, promising "another time, darling. You're too young to be a model for your father's art. He needs someone a little older, more knowledgeable. You are still unformed, innocent, young. You must wait," and then the door closed and Annabelle was left outside while her mother went back to pose for her husband.

Sometimes when Annabelle remembered that moment, she almost hated her mother. She had wanted her chance, and her mother wouldn't let her have it. Perhaps she should have argued or cried. She didn't want to wait. She wanted her father to see her *now*.

But Annabelle was a good child, an obedient daughter. Her mother said she must wait. Therefore, she would wait. If not for her father, then someone else—some other man who would be drawn to her like a moth to a candle. It would happen. Her mother had promised.

"But when?" and she was unaware she had spoken aloud until she saw Jules' raised eyebrows and understood he had not been following her thoughts.

"When will it happen? My mother," she explained awkwardly, twisting her hands together until the knuckles gleamed whitely in the lamplight, "my mother promised me a lover... someone like my father. She said I was beautiful, that men would follow me wherever I went. She used to call me her own 'lovely Annabelle.'

"Sometimes she would lie with me and twist our long hair together into one long rope, and you couldn't tell, not really, which was my mother's hair and which was mine. I was a pretty child then...'lovely Annabelle,'" and then she fell silent.

Lovely Annabelle she once was, but Anna was what she had become—the long curls cut short, the golden strands darkened and dirty-looking, the blue eyes washed to some indeterminate shade of gray.

There was no one left who remembered Annabelle, and no one who particularly cared about Anna. Although once, there had been a rose sent by a man she hardly knew who worked in the office next to hers.

"He brought me a rose," she said to Jules, "this man I didn't know. And I thought perhaps this was what my mother meant…that this flower would be the beginning of passion for me."

It was a full-blown red rose, tears of moisture still trapped on paper-thin petals. He had laid it on her desk before she came into the office, and at first, she didn't believe it was meant for her.

She lifted the stem, heavy with the weight of the blossom, and caressed her lips with the silken, scarlet petals. And deep inside her, a fire began to smolder, bringing an unaccustomed warmth and color to her pale cheeks.

"I put the rose in my water glass. I wanted it there, right in front of me, so I could see it while I worked"—typing endless meaningless reports about people she would never know.

All morning long, she typed, and while she worked, she cast furtive glances at the flower, fearing it might disappear before her eyes.

It didn't, of course, but what did happen was, in its own way, infinitely worse. The petals began to curl and the color to fade (She had failed to add water to the glass—and was that omission accidental or intentional?), and by the end of the day, the rose had withered before her eyes, the promise of passion gone before she could respond to it.

"Did the man come to see you?" Jules asked, leaning forward to see her more clearly. But Annabelle avoided his eyes.

"I like this office," she said instead. "It's never very bright in here. Bright lights hurt my eyes. My father's studio was bright. He said he needed light to see life more clearly. But sometimes it isn't good to see too much. It can hurt you."

But the light never hurt her father's eyes. And when Annabelle's mother was there, posing for one of the hundred—thousand!—pictures her father painted, the white light was shot through with color, as if her mother were a prism, capturing the clear beam and transforming it into all the colors of the rainbow.

"The man," Jules persisted, and Annabelle frowned. Man? What man? Oh, the man with the rose—Annabelle never knew his name, and now couldn't even recall his face or the color of his eyes or the shape of his mouth.

"He came by my desk as he was leaving," she answered finally, snatches of the long-ago conversation drifting through her memory like falling leaves.

"The rose," he had said hesitantly. "I hope you liked it. It's called Illusion. It made me think of you."

Annabelle looked again at the flower, but saw in its place the armfuls of roses her mother would gather from the bushes surrounding the house: the crimson-petaled Avon, the dark red Traviata, and her mother's favorite, the floribunda called Black Ice. She would slip the stems into her hair, thrust them deep into the neckline of her delicate silk gown, and then embrace her husband until the flowers were crushed and bleeding against her flesh.

The scent from those roses had filled the air, unlike this poor dead bloom, which had no scent, no life at all. Annabelle looked at the stranger—at his stooped shoulders and nails bitten to the quick—and couldn't even imagine being embraced by him, enfolded by those thin arms or crushed against that bony chest.

He is not a man like my father, she thought, remembering her father's muscular arms, covered with dark hairs curling with a life of their own. He is not a man at all, and in that moment, the stranger was lost.

"The flower died," she had said finally to the waiting man. (And why did he stay? Did he think she would want him?) With one thin finger, she tapped the bloom, and some of the petals drifted free from the heart.

"You brought me a flower with no life at all," and no longer seeing him, she methodically stripped off the rest of the petals.

It wasn't until there was a small pile of faded color in the center of her desk that she realized he had gone.

Then, almost unaware of what she was doing, she pressed one of the thorns—sharp even in death— against her fingertip, harder, harder, until a bubble of red appeared and fell onto the petals.

Annabelle wondered if someday she too would be so dried up that her blood would change like the color of the rose, from deep scarlet to a faded, brownish red.

"How could he say a dying flower reminded him of me?" she asked Jules angrily. "How dare he tempt me with passion only to offer death in the end?"

Jules swiveled his chair away from the light on his desk, until he was nothing more than a darker shadow in the darkness.

"Did you ever talk to him again?"

Annabelle shook her head, almost amused by the question. Talk to him? Why should she? She never even saw him again—although she supposed in the days and weeks that followed he must have passed her desk half a hundred times.

But he had ceased to exist for her. Her vision was taken up searching for the lover who was yet to come.

"You know, Anna, I can't help you if you won't talk to me." Jules' voice was sharp, cutting into her thoughts. "You want to be well again, don't you?"

"I was never sick," she answered, obstinate as a child when confronted with an unpleasant thought. "There's nothing wrong with me. Just because I want what my mother promised me... a man like my father... my father..."

Her words drifted off for a moment but she regained control.

"Someday my lover will come for me." *Someday my prince will come*—the words rose unbidden in her mind, from a fairy-tale perhaps? But her lover wasn't a fairy-tale prince or figment of her imagination. He was there, somewhere, waiting for her. She had only to be strong and hold on long enough, and he would find her.

And when he came, she would never be alone again.

Her mother had found her lover—the only lover she had ever wanted or needed—and stayed with him, though the passion burned her very soul. Annabelle could be as strong as her mother, couldn't she? Couldn't she?

"I think perhaps we should end this session," said Jules, setting down the gold-tipped pen with which he made notes each week. "There isn't much we can accomplish if you won't talk. You must face up to the reality of the past so you can you plan for your future. It is all very well to hope, Anna, to dream a little. But even dreams"—And did he really think she was listening to him?—"have to be grounded in reality."

The small brass desk lamp threw his elongated shadow on the ivory walls. As the evening drew on, his shadow grew larger, more powerful while his words drifted around Annabelle like snow in December, cold and smothering.

When Jules spoke so strongly, Annabelle was caught by his words, ensnared like a tiny bird by the movement of a deadly reptile. She couldn't move if she wanted to. Sometimes she would even find herself gasping for breath as though she had lost the ability to expand and contract her lungs.

Jules folded his hands—how strong they looked, clasped so firmly together—and fixed his eyes upon her.

Annabelle glanced at him and then away, the coldness of his gaze chilling her soul. Yet perversely, she wanted to stay here in his office, where the lights burned so softly. She was safe here. There was an air of timelessness, as though the world had stopped to allow her to catch her breath and find her strength.

And if Jules was cold to her—well, what of it? Her father had been cold; yet, when he focused that chilling, penetrating gaze on her mother, she ignited like a Roman candle, sparks shooting in every direction.

"I want to talk," she protested, but Jules shook his head.

"Next week, Anna." His words were less a promise than a price to be extracted from her—a pound of flesh each week until she was reduced to bone before his eyes. "When you come next week, we will talk together, you and I. I can help you, Anna," and the persuasiveness of his tone pulled at her. "If you work with me, we can uncover the truth. You want the truth, don't you, Anna?"

The truth—*did* she want the truth? What is truth? Pilate had asked, and whether he found the answer, no one ever said.

Annabelle knew the truth, but no one wanted to believe her. They would rather believe their own version of the past—an ugly, untrue, hurtful version. But Annabelle knew better. Annabelle could remember.

And there was enough time to recall the past, as she waited in her small empty room. It was so quiet— almost as quiet as it had been in her parents' house in the woods, where the silence was perfect and absolute. Even the blue jays knew better than to allow their raucous cries to disturb the peace required by her father and so jealously guarded by her mother.

Sometimes hours would go by with no one speaking at all, and when Annabelle finally used her voice, she would be surprised at the sound.

But color—the house had been filled with color. Metallic shades of gold and silver, deep pulsing reds and vibrant greens—every color known to man was captured by her father on large rectangles of white canvas.

And always, somewhere amidst the shades and hues, would be her mother, portraying whatever vision had seized her husband's mind. She would stand there—motionless, breathless, nearly lifeless—

while the brush stroked bits of her onto the canvas. Unmoving, until the vision released the artist, who, in turn, released his captive subject.

When Annabelle took her own apartment, she painted the walls and ceilings and floors white—stark white, bone white, the white of bleached driftwood tossed carelessly onto the shore after a storm.

And in the whiteness, she waited for someone to come, to bring all the colors of life alive through her.

"I couldn't do what my father did," she explained to Jules at the next session. "I couldn't create life from color as he did. So I thought if I took the color away, it would make it easier for someone else to bring it all to life. To start with a fresh canvas—clean, white, unused."

"You wanted to paint like your father?" Jules asked curiously. "Or did you just want to be like your father? He seemed a driven man, not easy to live with. Was your mother happy, Anna, living with a man so obsessed by his art?"

Annabelle frowned. How could Jules understand the man her father had been? How could anyone understand the driving force that held him in its grasp, forcing him to obey its every whim?

"When I was eight," she answered obliquely, forehead creased with the effort of memory, "my mother found a young fox caught in a trap at the edge of the woods."

Outside, the cold December sun gleamed fitfully through bare branches, but Annabelle felt again the warmth of a May morning and saw the sunlight dancing in her mother's hair and on the reddish brown fur of the injured animal cradled in her arms.

"She brought it up to the house, trailing bits of leaves behind her, and she didn't even notice her dress was smeared with its blood. I think she was going to bandage its leg. It was bleeding quite steadily… cut to the bone by the sharp teeth of the steel trap. Or perhaps it had tried to gnaw itself free…"

She closed her eyes for a moment as the agony of the trapped animal flooded through her. Trapped, with no means to escape except by inflicting more pain on an already bruised body.

Although sometimes, Annabelle thought, it was the only way.

"But just as she stepped through the French doors, my father saw her, and just as quickly wanted to paint her… the way my mother looked, carrying that poor suffering animal.

"It must have been near death by then. It didn't struggle, not even when my father twisted its head against my mother's breast and curled its bloodstained tail around her wrist.

"She stood there for nearly two hours, trapped in the act of entering her home just as the fox had been trapped, until my father was satisfied with what he had put on the canvas. Then he released her. But by then the fox had died in my mother's arms, while she stood patiently as my father painted her.

"He sold that picture for quite a bit of money, I think." Annabelle looked down at her hands, surprised to see she had been clenching them, surprised to see how wet they were with tears—why had she started to cry? It was only an animal after all, not nearly as important as her father's art.

"What did your mother do with the fox?" Jules asked softly.

Annabelle wiped the tears from her hands. She mustn't cry. She must not cry.

"She set it down on the loveseat in the corner," and Annabelle-the-child watched with what grace and tenderness her mother placed the bloody, lifeless body on the soft white cushions.

"Then she went to my father, who was so absorbed in his work that he never even noticed the fox had died. He was like that, you know," Annabelle explained, almost matter-of-factly. "When he was painting, nothing else mattered. It was just the way he was." She wasn't certain if she was explaining it to Jules, or the little girl and her mother, who both waited helplessly for his attention to leave the canvas.

"She pulled the neckline of her dress until the buttons released the fragile material and it fell like rain past her shoulders to the floor. My father looked up then. He saw my mother standing there, smears of blood on her shoulders and across her breast. Perhaps the fox had bit her in its agony.

"He ran his fingers lightly across the blood and then on the canvas, adding a touch of dark red to the painting. And then," Annabelle looked blindly out the window, "he reached for my mother. He never even knew when I left the room, just as he never knew when the fox had died.

"But it didn't matter," she added, forcing the words past a throat curiously constricted with pain. "After all, she was his wife and loved him so. And the picture kept the fox alive in a way. Nothing else mattered. Nothing."

"How did you feel about your mother allowing the fox to die?"

Annabelle looked at Jules in surprise. Didn't he understand? Her father had to paint, and nothing could be allowed to interfere.

"She had no choice," she answered hesitantly. "My father needed her to stand there with the fox, and my mother," Annabelle paused for a moment, searching for the right words to explain the strange symbiotic relationship that bound her parents, "my mother needed my father to need her. She would do anything, anything at all, for my father."

"Then why did she kill herself?" Jules swiveled in his chair until he was staring directly at Annabelle, forcing her to meet his eyes. Until now, he had been gentle, his words barely stroking her mind. He had a lover's touch—kind, persuasive.

But now, his rough words stripped away her memories, leaving her naked and defenseless in the cold light.

"She didn't kill herself," Annabelle answered mechanically, crossing her shivering arms in front of her chest.

It seemed as though she had been saying those words forever to a hundred different questioners. And none of them believed her. But she had to keep trying.

"We used to swim in that lake on warm summer evenings, my mother and I, while my father sat on the bank and painted her. And when she grew tired, she would float gently on the surface, her hair swirling in a golden cloud around her. My mother loved the water."

"But it was night, Anna, dark and cold. Why would your mother choose to swim alone in a cold lake unless she wanted to die?"

Annabelle shook her head. It wasn't true. It couldn't be true. The same words she had repeated to herself from the safety of her bedroom as she watched the stretcher carrying the slender wet figure. Only her mother's hair was exposed, slipping from under the cover to fall like a golden curtain to the ground. Poor dead drowned Ophelia, gone mad for love.

"It was a mistake. My mother would never have left my father. They needed each other!" and she struck the arm of the chair for emphasis.

Jules was silent but she knew that he, like all the others, didn't believe her. But Annabelle understood the truth. For whatever reason, her mother had left the house, and once outside, was forever prevented from returning, leaving behind a grieving child and an artist with no subject, no release.

"It was a mistake, an accident. She would not have left him. It was nobody's fault," but the last words were spoken without conviction.

Annabelle moved then, as though her body had just awakened from an unrestful sleep.

"I can't stay," buttoning her coat, pulling on her gloves. The dangers outside were preferable to those that awaited her here in the darkness. Too many questions, leading to doors that must remain closed— deep holes from which she could never escape— snares to twist her until she was caught forever.

It would be safer in her apartment, safer still in the house by the lake. Nothing could harm her there. If only she could escape.

January came, and with it, the first snowfall of the new year, soft and almost warm. Jules sat quietly for a time, and together they watched the snow drift down.

"It must have been difficult for you afterward. The house would be so empty with your mother gone," Jules observed finally, and Annabelle understood her respite was over. They would begin again. "You went away to school some weeks later, didn't you? Was it hard for you to leave your father? Did you miss him?"

Annabelle sat silently, watching the white flakes spin out of control. With her mother's death, what balance there had been to their lives was lost. Her father locked himself in the studio for days afterward, painting. And Annabelle drifted through the house, tall at thirteen, with the long golden hair so like her mother's. She would spend hours in her mother's bedroom, wrapping the familiar nightgowns and robes around her slender body, and look into the mirror, trying to find her mother's face in the glass.

It was two weeks later when her father emerged from his self-imposed isolation and, intent on the canvas he held, strode into his wife's room, only to find Annabelle seated at the dressing table, her mother's favorite red velvet robe pulled tightly around her.

For a moment, he stared in bewilderment, and then the familiar absorbed look came over his face as he studied the figure before him—the golden hair, the child's body, a woman's face.

And Annabelle, who had seen that look a thousand times before—and every time but once it had been directed at her mother—felt a curious mixture of fear and anticipation.

His fingers tightened on the paintbrush he still carried, and Annabelle knew he wanted to paint her—just her—and wouldn't rest until he did.

"I was afraid," she whispered now softly. "I knew what he wanted. But I couldn't, not again."

Her mother would have gone to the studio, Annabelle knew, and stood patiently while her husband tore bits of her free to lay on the canvas. But Annabelle was a child, not a woman, and the look in his eyes frightened her.

"I was not like my mother." The despair in her voice echoed in the room. How could she ever think she could be like her mother—inspire the kind of life and love and passion her mother had? She was a coward, poor weak Annabelle, so she ran away— away to school, leaving her father.

"Did you miss him, Anna?" Jules asked again.

After her mother's death, her father traveled to Europe, where he painted pictures of mountains and lakes. But never of people. Her father painted no more pictures of people—of women—of his wife.

"When he died, Anna, how did you feel?"

The room was cold, and Annabelle shivered. It was like a scene from a courtroom drama—a murder trial perhaps. *Where were you when the victim died? How did you feel—were you lost, grieving? Did you feel free?*

"I was alone in my apartment. My father's agent called, telling me of the plane crash and that my father had died." She stumbled a bit over the words, the way she had stumbled as she turned from the phone after resting it carefully in its cradle. The man's words, cut off in mid-sentence, echoed in the apartment: *"Dead. Dead."*

The phone had rung again, the shrillness shattering the silence. But Annabelle wouldn't answer it—not again. Not ever again. He wasn't coming home. She wouldn't have another chance.

"What did you do then?"

Annabelle frowned with the effort of remembering. What *had* she done? It seemed so long ago, although less than six months had passed. Late summertime it had been, and the leaves were just beginning to lose their fresh look as they died, cell by cell, on the trees.

Now it was the holiday decorations that were fading, and the snow, so clean and white, would soon be a dirty shroud on the city.

"Anna?"

She closed her eyes, unconsciously running the fingers of her right hand over the scar above her left wrist.

"I went into the kitchen and washed the cup I had used for coffee." And the pot and the silverware, and finally, every dish that lined the otherwise empty cabinet.

"I always clean up after myself. I don't like leaving messes for other people."

Her mother had left a mess—wet blankets dripping, a nightdress that, scrub as she would, Annabelle could never seem to make clean again.

A child, broken in pieces, never again to be whole.

But then, rules weren't made for people like her parents.

"And then?"

"I wanted a bath. I went into the bathroom and took off all my clothes so I could take a bath."

She had blocked the overflow outlet and when she finally lowered her thin naked body into the tub, some of the water cascaded onto the tile floor.

"I was so cold."

She remembered the coldness—the coldness of death. Her mother had left her; now her father was gone. And they had taken their world away with them, leaving her to stand out there alone, waiting. Watching. Wanting.

She had lain in the tub, inching her way down the porcelain interior until her knees were sticking out of the water, and her head was almost level with the surface, with her hair floating around her, the way her mother's had. Looking down, all she could see were her bony knees and the poor shriveled tips of her breasts, while all the rest of her body lay hidden.

It was peaceful and warm, and when she heard the phone, she turned the faucet handle more so the flow would be faster and drown its insistent ring, not caring that the water level had reached the top and was, even now, steadily trickling over the edge.

That was what had brought the landlady up two flights of stairs to Annabelle's door. The water had leaked through the floorboards to the apartment below.

When the knocking came, it was easy for Annabelle to disregard it. Her world was peaceful, calm. Nothing mattered anymore. The lake was warm.

"What did you do?" Jules' soft voice barely penetrated her consciousness.

"I just wanted to be left alone," she said. "I didn't want to see anyone. But they wouldn't leave me alone," and she didn't even try to explain who "they" were or why they would bother her.

"So you took the razor," Jules prompted, watching her narrowly through half-closed lids.

He looks like a lizard, Annabelle thought dreamily, waiting to flick his tongue to catch his dinner. But he won't catch me! she thought triumphantly, and suddenly sat up straight.

"It was my tub, after all!" she shouted. "My water! My apartment! My razor, my skin, my life! What right did anyone have to take it from me?" and the tears came, great tearing sobs pulling at her lungs until she was gasping for breath.

"She had no right!"

Annabelle had screamed at the landlady, who had used her passkey to open the door, only to find a tub full of rose-colored water. "No right! You have no right to come in here!" Words unheard, for the energy to change thought into sound had seeped from her as steadily as the blood had seeped from her veins.

"I wasn't her child! I wasn't anybody's child, not anymore!" and the sobs stopped as suddenly as they had begun, as Annabelle's words echoed in the room.

"Why did he leave me? I was ready. I wasn't afraid," and the words opened doors long closed.

It was late afternoon, and she had gone into her father's studio fresh from the lake, with only a towel wrapped around her swimsuit-clad body. Her father was painting yet another portrait of her mother.

"He always painted my mother. Oh, there were other things in the scene as well: animals, trees, the lake with the sun glancing off its surface to dazzle your eyes. But my mother was always there, irresistibly drawing your attention. I don't know what it was about my father's paintings that made her seem so alive. He'd been painting her for years, and she always looked the same: flaming eyes, golden hair, slender body..."

Annabelle's voice trailed off as she saw again the endless succession of pictures her father had created—some with her mother clothed in styles from long ago, some of her naked body gleaming like ivory, like bones.

Her father was in love with her mother's body—that much Annabelle-the-adult understood even if the child had been unable to perceive it at the time.

But was he in love with his wife?

"I never thought I would be as beautiful as my mother, even though she promised me my time would come. I grew taller, of course"—tall enough to reach first her mother's shoulders and then look into her eyes—"but to look like her seemed impossible. Still, our hair was the same, and I wore it long and loose like hers. I hoped I would look like her when I grew up."

But she hadn't. Something had gone wrong, it seemed, in those years after her mother's death. Like a plant denied the life-giving warmth of the sun, Annabelle had faded, her early promise just a bitter memory.

She got up from the office couch and walked to the small mirror hanging near the coat rack. The light in the room was dim but adequate, and Annabelle could see in the reflection the way her hair, now short and straight, failed to capture even a bit of glow from the lamp.

She ran her fingers impatiently through the strands, unsurprised to feel the brittleness of the ends. Like the hair on a corpse, she thought, and gathered a handful to pull it tightly back from her face. The skin stretched across her cheekbones, and it was a death's-head that stared back at her from the mirror.

"I'm not beautiful like my mother," she said aloud. "I never was, even at thirteen. He was wrong, you know," she added, turning back to Jules. "I wasn't ready, not then."

"Who was wrong, Anna?" Jules asked.

But her eyes were caught by the past, and she didn't see the desk and lamp and psychiatrist. There was only the sunlight and her father, and the empty canvas he had placed on the easel.

"Something different this time," he had murmured and began to sketch a waterfall, diamond flashes glittering on the whiteness. "Take off your suit," he added without turning, and Annabelle understood that he wanted to paint *her*, Annabelle, not her mother.

How long she had dreamed of her father wanting to paint her! And yet, now that the time had come, she resisted, fearing the moment when he would turn his life-draining gaze on her, reducing her to a mix of colors and shapes on the canvas.

But her father had to paint. Who was she to resist him?

It never seemed to bother her mother to undress in the studio, even though the air swirling through the French windows was cool. Her father liked to work in fresh air. He claimed it made the pictures sharper in his mind, but all Annabelle could think was how hard it must have been for her mother to stand in that chilly room for hours at a time, sometimes with nothing on at all to protect her body from the coldness.

This time, it was Annabelle whose flesh crawled with goose bumps in spite of the flush of embarrassment that suffused her skin. She had never before been naked in front of her father, and now, with her woman's body beginning to emerge from the childish curves of fat and flesh, she felt exposed. Unprotected. Unready for the close scrutiny her father gave her.

Yet, hidden in the back corners of her mind was the spark of satisfaction that this time it was *her* body her father wanted to paint—that it would be *her* face and eyes he would be capturing.

The spark grew, fanned to a flame each time her father's eyes raked over her. Gradually the chill left her body; she began to perspire, just lightly, a gentle moisture gathering under the hair lying on the back of her neck and beneath the soft curve of her barely formed breasts.

And she stood there, relaxing under his regard like a cat satiated by the rays of the sun.

"Turn a bit," he had commanded, but then, too impatient to wait, he adjusted her body himself, his hand lightly grazing the side of her neck. Annabelle flamed at his touch, desire bringing color to her cheeks. Unconsciously, she pulled her abdomen in a bit more and arched her narrow child's back to allow the light to stream across her chest.

And the pose, at first so foreign and uncomfortable, became easier to maintain as long as she looked into his eyes and saw herself as he did.

"Beautiful," she heard him say. For that alone she would have endured a thousand hours of the same pose. He picked up the brush and swirled the soft bristles in the oil before stroking it slowly on the canvas, and Annabelle imagined she could feel the silken tip caressing her skin.

Her father worked in silence, pausing every now and then to look at Annabelle before returning his gaze to the canvas. And each time she met his eyes, there was an exchange of the fire that once had existed only between her parents.

When he pulled her hair forward, his fingers brushed against her breasts, and the force of her feelings were almost more than she could bear. She wanted to move, just a little, toward him—but he had told her to stand still. Ever-obedient, she stood, though the fire threatened to consume her.

That was how her mother found them, just the two of them, the artist and his model.

"Anna? What are you thinking about, Anna?"

Annabelle looked at Jules blankly, not seeing him, but automatically answering his question, the question she thought she heard.

"It wasn't my idea." Was she answering Jules or defending herself against some unspoken accusation? "He said he needed a different model, someone pure and fresh and untouched..."

Her voice trailed off into the darkness, one hand covering her face, as though to hide behind the thin, splayed fingers. And she could still see the picture her father was painting—a waterfall and half-hidden behind it the figure of a young girl, with her long hair modestly covering her nakedness.

The rest of the painting was unfinished, incomplete—like the young model posing for it. But in the eyes her father had captured some essence of forbidden knowledge that belied the child-like body, hinting at the woman waiting behind half-closed lids.

"My mother just stood there and watched him for a time—it seemed like hours, forever..." Forever, before her father stilled his brush and looked absently at his wife, as though she wasn't there, not really—as though all that mattered was Annabelle.

The look caught her mother with the force of a blow that stripped the skin from her face and left the nerve ends quivering with the pain of rejection.

"It wasn't my idea," she said again to Jules.

And yet, Annabelle had gone into the studio when he was alone. She had stood there, in her thin bathing suit, willing him to see her.

But not for the world would she have hurt her mother.

"She was right for this picture," her father said finally, looking at Annabelle critically before applying the faintest caress of soft brown to the undercurve of the belly of the painted Annabelle. "Young and tender, too young for you to model."

Annabelle still believed he never intended to be cruel, only honest.

"I think," he added, scrutinizing the canvas dispassionately before gazing at Annabelle's mother, "this may be the beginning of a whole new series."

There was silence in the room after that, except for the gentle stroking of the brush against the canvas and the uneven breathing of Annabelle's mother.

And Annabelle, barely breathing, was still as a statue—cold now and ashamed, wanting only to hide her nakedness and return to the safety of a world where she could watch her parents twist and turn against their need for each other.

Perhaps her mother had understood and forgiven Annabelle the part she had played, all unknowing. She saw the painter engrossed in his work and the fresh child's body capturing his attention, and silently left the room. After all, nothing should interrupt his work. That was all that mattered.

The draft from the open windows cut across Annabelle's unprotected back. She trembled uncontrollably until her father threw down his brush in disgust.

"I can't paint if you won't stand still! Leave! We'll finish it tomorrow," he said angrily, before turning to stare moodily out the window.

Annabelle ran from the studio to her room where she sat at her window and watched her mother swimming in the cold lake. With every stroke her mother took, with every wave that broke across her mother's back, Annabelle shivered in sympathy.

And the fire that had burned so unbearably within her was reduced to ashes.

Annabelle had fallen asleep at the window, her forehead resting on the glass. It wasn't until the next morning that she understood the full extent of her mother's love for her father.

"She left him that quickly because of me," Annabelle said now to Jules, "and then I left him, too. I was afraid.

"But I thought that, when I was older, when I saw him again... I didn't want to let him down. My mother wouldn't have. She was strong. I would be strong, too."

"Anna, it's over now. It was wrong of your father to paint you, wrong of your mother to take her own life—"

But Annabelle stopped Jules, throwing up her hands as though to ward off the words, the accusations, the implication. "How can you say that? All that mattered was my father's art! My mother died for him!"

And Annabelle was caught between the two of them, ripped apart. Bleeding. Dying.

"Anna," Jules started, but she was lost to him, to the unbearable present. She caught up her coat and vanished through the office door, wanting only to reach her apartment, to find her past, to make her peace.

"I never meant to hurt you, Mother."

The words echoed in the empty room, although she couldn't remember walking home or unlocking the door.

"I just wanted him to look at me for once. I just wanted someone to want me," and she shook her head slowly as she saw herself reflected in the window.

How could she have ever thought she was as beautiful as her mother? She was ugly, and tearing off her clothes, she saw the shriveled skin across her chest, the dull hair hanging limply about her head, the eyes, large and staring and devoid of life.

"If my father saw me now, he wouldn't want to paint me," and there was relief in the thought. If they were all together again in the house by the lake, nothing could go wrong. Her father would paint only her mother, and Annabelle could stay safely in the background.

"Mother?"

Her voice was uncertain in the darkness. Where had her mother gone? Why had she left her now just when Annabelle needed her most? She was just a child after all—a good child—an obedient child who was only doing what she had been told.

"It was all a mistake," she said loudly, hoping her mother would hear her, out where she was swimming in the lake.

Annabelle stepped closer to the window, wanting to catch her mother's eye. But perhaps she was too high up—on the third floor of the apartment building—the second story of the house by the lake, watching her mother swim with strong sure strokes through the sparkling water.

She undid the latch and the cold winter wind gusted in, but Annabelle didn't shiver. Why should she? It was June and the sun was shining, and there was her mother, far out on the lake, and her father, carrying his easel down to the shore.

He was going to paint her mother as she floated on the water, and Annabelle could watch from the safety of her bedroom window.

"Annabelle! Annabelle!"

Her mother's voice called to her, warm and loving and full of forgiveness. And her upraised arm glittered with drops of water in the sunlight.

"I don't want to be alone up here," Annabelle said aloud, slipping her hand through her hair, feeling with the fingers of memory each golden curling strand. And then, with one final movement, she shook her long hair across her shoulders before running to them.

Author's Notes

The stories in this collection were not methodically planned out but rather, came unbidden and when least expected.

Something would trigger the idea—an overheard bit of conversation, an interaction between two strangers, an item left behind when no longer wanted or needed—and my writer's mind would seize on it, layering words around it the way an oyster secretes nacre around a bit of grit.

In the oyster's case, that coating serves to protect the mollusk's soft inside from any further discomfort. In *my* case, words serve the same purpose. The story trigger is the irritant, and I have learned that I have to do *something* with it or continue to be aggravated by it.

Not being a patient, long-suffering person, I chose to write, hoping to produce pearls or at least, something better than the grit that started it all.

About Nancy Christie

Nancy Christie has a passion for fiction and has been making up stories since she was a child, engaging in "what if" and "let's pretend" activities that took her far beyond her northeastern Ohio home.

Her short stories have appeared in print and online magazines, including *Ariel Chart, Two Cities Review, Streetlight Magazine, Talking River* and *The Chaffin Journal,* among others. Several of her stories have earned contest placement or awards.

She writes fiction because "I love the world of make-believe. I love learning about my characters, following them as they live their lives, rejoicing with them when things go well and commiserating with them when life becomes painful and events are almost unendurable. Crazy? Maybe. But you have to be a little crazy to spend your days and nights with people only you can see and hear."

For more information about Nancy Christie go to her website: www.nancychristie.com, read her blogs (One on One, The Writer's Place, and Focus on Fiction), or follow her on social media:

Twitter: @NChristie_OH
Facebook: @NancyChristieAuthor
Goodreads: (www.goodreads.com/NancyChristie)

About the Press

Unsolicited Press is a small publisher in Portland, Oregon that published poetry, fiction, and creative nonfiction written by award-winning and emerging authors.

Learn more at unsolicitedpress.com